THE HIGHLANDER'S REBELLIOUS BRIDE

HIGHLAND LEGACIES

AILEEN ADAMS

THE HIGHLANDER'S REBELLIOUS BRIDE
BOOK ONE OF HIGHLAND LEGACIES

Rowan Campbell's not even remotely interested in being a bride. Yet her father insists that this untamed, fiery daughter of his have a husband, so Rowan devises a plan. A competition. As a competent archer she's more than willing to put her skills against the ablest of bow hunters in the realm.

Lachlan McDonald's known—and loved—Rowan since she was a wee lass, when he first arrived at her father's keep to be a guard. He's watched her grown into a beautiful woman who refuses to be tamed. Now he has a chance to compete to win this woman's heart and hand.

1

———

Late Summer

"A ll may be seated," the rector said as the bride and groom stood at the altar of the church, eyes only for each other.

Rowan Campbell was sitting in the second pew from the front and was trying, rather unsuccessfully, to reconfigure her dress in such a way that it was no longer sucking the very breath from her lungs. But try as she might, no matter how she wiggled, she couldn't fix it. If anything, her fidgeting was only making her corset dig even more deeply into her ribs.

How do women wear these, day in and day out? she wondered, wishing she were back in her normal outfit of a wool skirt, shirt, and casaquin. It was perfect for roaming the forest and braes, allowing her to move freely, unlike the constricting bit of frippery she had on now.

"Stop moving," her best friend, Blair MacManus, whispered to her. "Ye'll attract attention."

Rowan looked over and saw that Blair seemed far more comfortable than she in her finery, but then, that was often the case. Blair was the calm to Rowan's storm and had always been so, ever seen since they first became friends as children. Blair had her mother's quiet temperament. Mary MacManus was the area's midwife and healer, and Rowan often thought that her soothing voice alone was palliative enough to help the area's women through even the most harrowing of births.

Rowan turned back toward the altar and watched as her sister, Kirsty, recited something to her betrothed, Robert MacKenzie. He was laird to a large castle to the far north, and Kirsty would be traveling with him the next day to her new home.

Rowan's father, Laird Fergus Campbell, had arranged the marriage, but in the time that Laird Robert had been traveling to Castle Morcoille to negotiate the terms of the marriage, Kirsty had fallen in love with him, or so she professed to anyone who would listen. Rowan was not among those people, of course. She had no time for love or marriage or for those who spent their days obsessing over it.

But she does look happy, Rowan reminded herself as her sister's face erupted into a beatific smile. Laird Robert's lips began to move, reciting the words that would bind them to each other forever.

"Laird Robert's brother is quite handsome, is he nae? And I hear he is unmarried," Blair muttered to Rowan sometime later, when the two were seated at one of the many tables in the castle's banquet hall, surrounded on all sides by revelers celebrating the union.

Laird Robert's family, including his brother Stuart, had traveled down with him to attend the wedding.

Rowan looked over to where Stuart MacKenzie was seated at a nearby table, making one of the village girls laugh prettily. His thick brown hair was tossed carelessly over one eye, and his smile was devilishly charming.

"He looks like a scoundrel to me, and besides, even if he were a saint, I would nae have him."

Blair rolled her eyes. "Och, Rowan, are ye really

so set on being alone for the rest of yer life? With no husband or children to take care of?"

"Aye. I'll have a whole village of people to heal, and I'll hunt when I can and sell what I catch. Donnae worry about me, Blair. I have a plan."

"Sounds like a lonely plan to me, lassie," Blair said, tipping her head in that way Rowan knew meant she was trying to reason with her.

But Rowan was not a woman easily reasoned with, and so she stood up from her seat and walked toward one of the tables laden with food.

The castle kitchens had outdone themselves that night; there were enough roasted pheasants to feed all of Scotland, as well as potatoes in every variation. It was a bowl of potatoes roasted in duck fat that caught Rowan's eye, and she made her way toward it, stopping a moment on her way to listen as a group of musicians nearby began to tune their instruments, preparing for the ceilidh dancing that would soon occur.

But soon enough, her ravenous stomach pushed her toward the table, where the golden potatoes awaited her. Smiling to herself, for they were one of her favorite foods, she picked up the serving utensil and began to pile her plate high with the delicious morsels.

She was so involved in her task that she did not notice the presence at her side until it, or rather, *he* spoke.

"Are ye going to leave any roasties for the rest of us, or take them all yerself, lass? It would nae be fair, ye ken, for ye are treated to such delicacies every day of the week, while the rest of us must suffer through gruel."

Rowan looked up and into the bright green eyes of Lachlan Stewart, a castle guard whose presence never failed to vex her. Lachlan was handsome, aye, but he was also frustrating, taking great pleasure in teasing Rowan at every opportunity. He teased her like a younger sister, yet sometimes, she could swear he looked at her in much the same way that Robert looked at Kirsty.

"I'll take as many as I like, and ye can stop lying about the food yer served on a daily basis, which ye and I each ken is fit for a man far better than yerself," Rowan said, punctuating her point with a final spoonful of potatoes, resulting in a tower that wobbled precariously on her plate.

"Aye, 'tis true, lass, the food here is fine," Lachlan said with a laugh.

"Donnae call me lass, Lachlan Stewart. 'Tis the laird's daughter I am. And prefer to be addressed as such," Rowan bit back, her fingers tightening around her plate, turning her knuckles white.

"Aye, ye are the laird's daughter. And yet sometimes," he said, tapping his chin with a long finger, his eyes crinkled with mischief as he leaned close and whispered, "I would swear ye were closer to an animal than a woman, with the way ye act."

He punctuated his joke by grabbing the serving spoon out of Rowan's hand and helping himself to his own small mountain of the roasted, golden brown morsels, his eyes never leaving hers as he did so.

"At least I donnae look like an animal. If ye let that beard grow anymore, the farmers will mistake ye for a highland cow," Rowan told him, reaching out and pulling on the beard covering his jaw. It was soft to the touch and warm, and Rowan snatched her hand back so suddenly she upset her balance, steadying herself with a hand to the table.

Lachlan squinted, and Rowan could see he was preparing a witty response, but she did not let him utter it. Instead, she walked away, the long skirt of her emerald-green velvet dress trailing behind her.

She exhaled slowly as she sat back down at the table, a small but victorious smile on her lips as she pulled her chair in and picked up a fork.

"What just happened there? Lachlan looks ready to spit fire, and yer wearing a grin like ye've stolen the last biscuit from the tin," Blair said, her eyes darting between Rowan, who was placidly chewing potatoes, and Lachlan, who was now looking at them from his stance by the fireplace, where some of the other guards were jesting with each other as they enjoyed the free-flowing ale.

"Just Lachlan being a bampot. Nothing new," Rowan said, shoving another large forkful of potatoes in her mouth and chewing. She kept her eyes trained on her plate, but she could feel Lachlan's eyes still on her, his sharp green gaze tracking her like he was the hunter and she was prey.

2

Early Winter

Lachlan's breath was coming out in cloud-like puffs, the pre-dawn chill creeping between the fibers of his kilt and coat. He did not like the morning guard shift, but he was not alone in this; there wasn't a guard among the fifty employed by the laird who relished having to get up in the dark of winter and slowly traverse the frozen ground. At this time of year, the sun didn't rise 'til gone eight o'clock, and even then, its rays were hardly enough to warm a nose, let alone a whole body. It was pure misery.

But there was one benefit to walking the grounds this early that made the experience worth the discomfort, and it, or rather she, was now striding across the grounds toward the castle's armory.

Rowan.

Her long braid of chestnut brown hair was swishing behind her as she walked purposefully toward the armory. Lachlan couldn't quite make out her facial expression in the dark, but he could imagine it well enough—her brow furrowed in thought, her plump, soft pink bottom lip tucked between her teeth absentmindedly. It was her studious face, her serious face, one she only wore when she was out here in the early morning, preparing to practice archery.

Lachlan wasn't sure how long she had been sneaking out of the castle to practice wielding a bow and arrow, but he had first seen her months ago. That morning, he had watched in awe as she ran, quick and graceful as a cat, away from the castle's kitchen entrance and over the grounds, moving so fast it seemed her feet barely touched the earth.

She had sped right past where he was stationed next to the armory, its outer wall hiding him from view but giving him a perfect vantage point to see the castle's west side, which backed up to the forest.

Rowan had always been strange, surprising, unlike any other lass he had ever met, so he should not have been nearly so shocked when she walked out of the armory with a quiver of arrows and a bow slung over her shoulder and strode confidently toward the practice ground, the line of painted targets visible even in the winter darkness.

She'd shown natural skill that day, her hands holding the bow as though she'd done it a thousand times before, and since then, she had only grown better.

After that first day, Lachlan had taken as many morning shifts as he could, switching with the other guards, who were more so happy to avoid the cold, grey mornings that they did not question his motivations. Each time he rose and imagined the frigid air slowly stiffening his shoulders and numbing his hands, he remembered that as soon as he saw Rowan, a warmth unparalleled by that following a dram of whisky or a hot bath would settle over him, permeating to his very soul as he watched her shoot arrow after arrow and hit the center of the target, every single time.

She had more talent than all the guards combined, except him, for no one could beat him. It was a well-known and tested fact. He couldn't count the number of guards that had challenged him to a contest over the years and, when he easily bested them, been forced to offer up whisky and coin as penance for being foolish enough to underestimate him.

Now, Lachlan watched as Rowan strode out of the castle's back entrance and ran to get the smaller bow and the arrows with the red fletching that she preferred.

How long would it take me to best her? he wondered to himself.

After all, she might be good, but she was still a lass, and he was a castle guard with years of training. He was also the best hunter for miles, well-known for being able to shoot down a red deer from one hundred paces away, piercing its head and killing it quick and clean. He doubted Rowan had ever shot anything other than the target she was walking towards now.

She walked as though sure she were the only person awake in the world this early, as though there could be no possible chance of someone catching her. But Lachlan knew better and looked around him, making sure they were alone. Because she had nearly been caught, once, and it was only because of him that she was able to continue her twice-weekly archery exploits.

It had happened last spring. Lachlan had lost

track of time that morning and had been surprised to see the other guards stomping down the grass toward him, ready to take over his shift. He had watched in muted horror as Rowan looked over her shoulder, searching for the source of the noise. She hadn't waited for the guards to step into view. Instead, she had dropped her bow and arrow and sprinted out of sight, running faster than Lachlan would have thought possible in a dress.

When the guards came to a stop near Lachlan's perch on the armory wall, Bernard, one of the newer recruits, had nodded at the bow and arrow.

"I thought ye preferred the arrows with the blue fletching? Because 'tis one of the colors in yer father's clan tartan?" the lad had asked, his voice wavering with the unsteadiness born of adolescence.

Lachlan had nearly smiled at the lad for remembering such a small detail he had told in passing, but instead, he grunted and lied, telling them he had wanted to see if the red fletching might serve him better.

The authority he had over the men had kept them from asking any more questions, and he had stridden to gather the bow and arrow himself as they looked on. He hoped Rowan had not run into anyone as she stole back into the castle. It was wrong, but he didn't want their mornings together to end.

If he were doing his duty, he would have turned her in to her father long ago, after that first morning when he spotted her out in the fields. It was dangerous for a lass to play with weapons, especially the laird's favorite daughter. But Lachlan knew that even if he did tell the laird about Rowan's morning exploits, there was a good chance Rowan would still be out there in the practice ground the next morning.

The laird doted on Rowan, never admonishing her for her adventurous exploits. She was the most energetic of his five daughters, and as the youngest, she got away with it all. Her father was far too busy with running the castle and looking after its people to notice his daughter's mischievous ways. Had Rowan's mother lived past the bout of influenza she contracted when Rowan was five, perhaps the lass would have grown up to be a proper lady like her sisters. But as it was, Rowan was like a storm, unpredictable and uncontainable.

Lachlan watched now as she took the proper position, twenty yards from the target.

She pushed her braid over her shoulder, letting it fall down her back where it ended just above her waist and was tied with a bit of blue ribbon. She wore the more comfortable clothing she preferred, a plain dress and casaquin with a knit scarf to shield her neck against the worst of the biting wind that whistled through the trees on the edge of the forest.

Lachlan remembered the dress she had worn to her sister Kirsty's wedding, a bright green the exact same shade as the braes rising up on the castle's north side. She had looked like a lady that night, but her words were still that of a spitfire, her barbs sharp as the arrow now leaving her bow and burying its head into the center of the target.

A smile slowly crept over Rowan's face, and Lachlan could not help but mirror it, glad once again to have this time with her. This secret.

3

———

"Enough, Rowan. 'Tis all gone on long enough," Rowan's father thundered at her the moment she walked into his study.

She was so surprised at his raised voice that for a moment, she stood frozen in the doorway, unable to speak, even though she knew the reason behind the fury reddening his bearded cheeks and lighting a fire in his normally tranquil eyes.

She shouldn't have been so shocked. After all, her maid Ainslee had warned her, rushing at her the moment she entered her room mid-morning after a sojourn to the woods to pick mushrooms with Blair.

"Yer father is angry as a hare caught in a trap," she had rasped, tugging Rowan into the room and shutting the door.

"Whatever for?" Rowan had asked, though she had her suspicions, which Ainslee confirmed.

"He's found out ye've been going out in the mornings. What were ye thinkin', going out by yerself before dawn when all manner of mischievous creatures, both man and otherwise, are about?" Ainslee had exclaimed, rolling her eyes even as she ushered Rowan to the tub she had already filled with near-boiling water, begging Rowan to undress and bathe quickly, for her father was expecting her as soon as possible in his study.

That was a mere half hour ago, and in that time, Rowan had prepared herself for a slight chastising by her father, before eventually being forgiven and allowed to continue to practice archery, perhaps with a guard at her side. It would be annoying, but she could bribe the man to leave her easy enough, as long as it wasn't Lachlan. Not everyone was as principled as he.

Coming back to the room, Rowan wished her father had opened one of the windows at the far wall. His glare, combined with the heat of the fire coming from the hearth, had caused a subtle sheen of anxiety to form at her back.

"Get in and close the door, lass," her father ordered her, and she acquiesced, taking a seat on the chair across from him, her side facing the hearth.

He looked slightly taken aback that she agreed so easily. Rowan was not in the habit of taking orders from people, after all, but she hoped that her obedience would play in her favor.

"I'm sorry, Father," she began, clearing her throat and raising her eyes to meet her father's. "I swear I'm always careful, always, and—"

"I donnae care for yer apologies, lass," he interrupted her. "'Tis one thing to go off in the woods with Blair and the widow MacManus to gather berries and mushrooms at midday. 'Tis another entirely to be found early in the morning, all alone by the forest. One of the guards saw ye at no later than eight o'clock this morning, walking into the woods all alone, vulnerable as a child in a fairy tale," her father began without preamble.

Rowan frowned, confused. Wasn't this about her archery? If so, why was he talking about her picking mushrooms this morning?

"Did ye nae think about yer safety?" he continued, leaning close to her, his voice lowering, his tone growing more serious with every word. "Did ye nae wonder what might befall ye, out there on yer own? What was so important that had ye disappearing into the woods just as the sun was rising? Why must ye act like this, lass, like yer some foundling, rather than one of the most important people in this entire castle, and a lady, as well?"

Though his questions hurt, she did not understand them, at least not at first. It was only after sitting a few moments in tense silence that Rowan understood.

I'm nae being admonished for archery. I'm being admonished for going mushroom hunting this morning.

She couldn't help the smile of relief that took over her face, but she immediately regretted it when she looked up and saw her father glaring at her.

"Och, is this funny to ye, lass?" he shouted so loud that she winced.

Rowan shook her head, about to speak.

Her father wouldn't let her, his voice tight as he said, "Laugh all ye like, lass, but ken this morning was yer last outing. Yer nae to go out alone anymore. Nae more healing. Nae more pickin' flowers and berries and whatever else stains yer hands and dresses and makes the laundry maids so vexed. Leave it to the MacManuss. Ye have yer own duties to attend to. Yer going to finally start acting like the lady ye were bred to be."

Rowan blanched at this.

He didn't breed me to be a lady. He didn't breed me to be anything. He always let me do whatever I wanted, she thought angrily.

Her father had never placed the same expectations on her as he had her sisters. She was the youngest, a surprise baby that occurred when her mother was forty and thought to be past child-bearing age. Her mother had done her best when Rowan was young, but after she died, her father had given up trying to tame her. It had been clear even back then he was already tired from caring for her sisters, securing them tutors who could teach them to be polite and demure, to embroider and sing and dance in order to impress the husbands her father had selected for them, who would whisk them away to a far-off keep to have bairns and become ladies of their own castles.

Rowan had thought she had escaped such a fate. She had been allowed to engage tutors in whatever subjects she liked, preferring history and Latin to her sisters' literature and French. She had stopped wearing fine clothing when she was twelve, assenting to it only for the most important occasions, and even then, she and Ainslee had fought bitterly each time she was forced into stays and petticoats.

Mary MacManus had started teaching her the healing arts when she was thirteen, and Rowan's father had barely noticed when she disappeared for entire days into the woods. She had thought they had an understanding, an unspoken agreement about the way she would be allowed to live her life— namely, however she pleased.

Clearly, I've been mistaken, she thought with an internal groan.

"Rowan Campbell. Are ye listening to a word I'm saying? Make nae mistake, lass, none of this is said in jest, so ye best keep yer ears open," her father roared, and Rowan's head snapped up quickly, her eyes meeting her father's ones.

"Aye, Father. I hear ye, clear as a bell," she said, her voice far softer than normal and absent all its usual power.

She had been a shadow of herself from the moment she stepped into the room, trying to placate his rage. It didn't feel right. None of this did. Not her whispering like a church mouse, nor her father yelling at her, which until today he'd never done, not even on the day she'd ruined a brand new dress with mud and berry stains from a day spent picking brambles with Blair.

Even the clothes on her back made her feel out

of sorts; instead of her serviceable, sturdy frock and boots, she was dressed in a long, berry-colored wool dress with a ruffled fichu at her neck. Ainslee had insisted on stockings, tied at the thigh with a ribbon, and shoes that made it impossible for her to walk at anything except a snail's pace.

Ainslee had chided Rowan as she helped her wash and dress, shoving her into a corset tied tight enough that Rowan swore she could hear her lungs squeal in protest every time she moved.

"Though I dinnae ken what ye were thinking, I do ken this—yer father will nae be nearly so cross with ye if ye show up looking like a proper lass and remind him yer capable of more than covering yerself in mud and thorns," Ainslee had said as she yanked Rowan's curls into place, pinning them tight enough to make Rowan's scalp ache.

Reaching up now, Rowan touched the intricate, coiled bun at the back of her head, taming her wild curls into submission the same way it appeared her father wanted to tame her.

Rowan was suddenly reminded of Lachlan's words at her sister's wedding the previous year when he had told her she was often more animal than woman.

She had never seen a problem with the way she

acted. She knew she was different, but she thought that was what her father had loved about her. She was so unlike her sisters, from her dark hair—a stark contrast to their auburn tresses—to her interests. None of her sisters had ever taken much stock in playing outside, while Rowan had, according to stories from Ainslee's mother, her nursemaid, attempted to run to the forest the moment she could put one foot in front of the other.

Her father must have seen her questioning herself, doubting herself and his love for her, for he leaned toward her and put a hand to her head, a gesture of affection he had done since she was a wee bairn.

"I've always kenned ye were different than yer sisters, and I allowed it because yer me favorite," he told her, his voice growing quieter, losing the ferocity of only moments before. "I ken a father is nae supposed to play favorites, but how could I nae, when ye were so like yer mother as a bairn," he said, laughing to himself.

Rowan felt her chest warm at her father's pronouncement.

"Even now, I see her strength in ye. Yer stubborn just like she was."

Rowan smiled at the mention of her mother. She

had few memories of her, but those she did she trea-sured like the finest jewels—the feel of her mother's fingers as she untangled her hair, her rose and honey smell, the dimple on the left side of her mouth that was mirrored in Rowan's own face.

"She was stubborn?" Rowan asked, hoping her father might use the question to relay some unknown story about the mother she knew so little about.

"Aye. She refused me proposal three times before we were finally wed, and she always had to do things her way."

"Just like me," Rowan whispered.

"Exactly like ye," her father said, dropping his hand from her head and sitting back in his chair.

"But," he began, and Rowan looked up at that, her stomach dropping with the intuition she had honed from years of observing her surroundings, as a hunter should.

"She was still a lady, lass. She still knew how to behave. I've failed in teaching ye that. I've doted on ye too long, and now, enough is enough."

4

———

Rowan's eyes flitted to her father's face, trying and failing to read his expression and glean something of what he was about to say to her. Anxiety crept into her legs, and she could feel them quaking beneath her skirts.

She never shook. She might be spirited, fiery even, but she prided herself on never reacting to distress. It was a skill she had honed from her time spent with Mary MacManus, who had learned to keep her temper even during the most troubling situations.

"A midwife and healer must always remain calm, lass, else all will go up in smoke."

Rowan tried to repeat this to herself now, but Mary's words did not help her as they normally did, and she could feel her hands start to shake as well as her father opened his mouth and said three words she had never expected to hear.

"Yer getting married."

"I'm... what... how..." she sputtered, a thousand questions clouding her mind, making it impossible to utter a full sentence.

"Yer getting married," her father repeated slowly, his words measured. "This season. By the time the crocuses are out, there will be a band on that wee finger of yers, and ye'll have a husband to occupy yer time."

Crocuses, traditionally seen as the first sign of spring, were due to pop out of the ground in a matter of weeks.

"There'll be nae more disappearing into the woods with Blair and the widow MacManus to collect grass and flowers. 'Tis time for ye to act like a laird's daughter, with all that entails."

"Act like a laird's daughter when ye have nae raised me to be such? When ye have let me lead me own life these past eighteen years? What has suddenly changed yer mind, Father?" Rowan asked, her anxiety ebbing, replaced with anger and confusion.

It felt good to be angry, to feel the strength of the

emotion flood her, settling her quakes and allowing her to once again sit tall, her shoulders thrown back and her chin high.

Her father faltered, clearly having expected his proclamation to stun her into silence.

This allowed Rowan to continue her tirade.

"And they're nae grasses and flowers that Iona and I gather," she shouted. "Well, I suppose some of them are, but we gather herbs, too, all of which are used to keep the people of yer castle and its surrounding lands healthy. Iona and Mary heal them, and I so do I. I'm trained as a healer, Father. Enough to be able to make me own way in the world with me knowledge. I can support meself. I will nae need a husband to look after me, when I can do it far better meself. And I donnae want a husband, either, as I'm sure ye can well ken."

Rowan's voice had risen with each word she spoke, and at last, as she finished speaking, she sat back in her chair, her chest heaving with exertion, feeling a creeping sense of victory. Her father had not said anything, but there was a war of emotions on his face, and previous circumstances told her that very soon, he would accept her words and agree with her. It was always easier that way.

Her father's face suddenly softened from its

blankness, and he rose from his chair and came to kneel before her, his knee cracking as it touched the floor. Bracing one arm on the bent leg in front of him, with his other, he reached out and grasped Rowan's hand in his.

"I'm sorry, lass. I've done ye wrong. I should nae have let ye roam around on yer own thinking that was the way things would always be, for it is nae. It is nae the way, lass."

His voice was so gentle, his look so kind, that Rowan's eyes began to burn with tears. "I'm sure yer a very skilled healer, lass, but it cannae be yer liveli-hood. Lairds' daughters donnae spend their lives as healers. They spend them as wives and mothers. It is how it has always been done, me dearest Rowan."

Rowan could feel her face threatening to crum-ble, the sadness beginning to overwhelm her. She tried to tug her hand from her father's, needing to cover her face and shield him from her tears, but his grip was far stronger than hers.

"I ken 'tis hard, lass, but 'tis yer fate and ye must accept it. It was wrong of me to try and keep ye from it for so long. I've grown soft-hearted in me old age, but yer mother would smite me from heaven if she knew I'd let ye spend yer whole life alone."

Rowan nodded, letting the tears fall as she

shrunk back in her chair, bowing her head until her gaze rested on her father's hand, engulfing her own.

"It might nae be so bad, Rowan," her father whispered to her. "Ye might even take to being married."

Rowan chuckled, for there could be nothing she would dislike more than being chained to a man for all eternity, forced to cede his every whim and directive.

"I'll choose the man, and he'll be good and kind and will treat ye well. Ye might be so lucky as to grow to love him. Like yer mother and I did one another."

Rowan shook her head, knowing that love like that did not happen every day and most certainly not in arranged unions. Her parents had had a love marriage, one that destiny itself had crafted.

I will nae be so lucky, she thought, a rueful smile touching her lips.

Her father said nothing more, but his other hand came to cup her cheek as he leaned forward, pressing a soft, paternal kiss to her forehead.

They sat in silence for some time, her father no doubt enjoying the rare sight of his daughter acquiescing, and Rowan formulating a plan in her head, for she would not sit here and simply swallow her father's orders.

He wants to see me married by spring? Fine. But I

shall do it me own way, she thought as she stood up, dislodging his hands from hers. Her father stood as well.

Rowan turned to him, fists on her hips, and announced, "I will choose me own husband. I want to find someone…" she halted, hating that she was about to lie, but knowing there was no other option. "Someone I can love, as ye say. But I will nae leave it up to chance. I donnae have faith in chance, but I do have faith in meself and me own judgment. So let me choose me husband, and I will agree to marry by the time the crocuses have sprung."

And I'll choose a man who will accept me as I am, she thought privately to herself. She did not care about love, but she did care about her happiness. She would not be saddled with some dullard who wanted to hide her away in a house with their bairns, sequestering her to a life where the only contact she had with the outdoors was through the plated glass of a window.

"Of course, Rowan. I trust ye to choose correctly, and I'm glad ye agree to me plan. I kenned ye would see reason. Yer mother would be proud of ye, lass," her father said, kissing her hand.

Rowan winced at the mention of her mother,

wondering whether she would have appreciated Rowan's subterfuge.

Father did say she had to do things her own way. Maybe her mother would understand, Rowan thought as her father walked her to the door and bid her good afternoon, a wider smile on his face than she had seen in some time.

It almost made her feel guilty about what she was planning.

Almost.

5

———

'll meet ye in a few days at the games, son. I
cannae wait to see how ye have grown.

Lachlan's eyes scanned the letter again, rereading the familiar swirls of his father's neat, quick handwriting. Though he had received the letter only yesterday, he had read it half a dozen times now, the folds in the paper already growing soft from so much handling.

His father, Seamus Stewart, was a tall, broad man of five and fifty years of age with whitening hair and an easy smile that rarely left his face. His eyes were the same as Lachlan's, a bright, verdant green, and he had passed on to Lachlan his quick wit and ease of laughter as well.

But as alike as they were, Lachlan rarely saw his

father. He had been sent to the Campbell keep as a lad of just twelve to train as a guard, and since then, he had spent but a few days a year with his father. Seamus always came to the annual clan games, and Lachlan traveled back to his clan lands if there was a family wedding or funeral, but the rest of the year, they communicated by letter.

It wasn't an unusual arrangement to send a lad off to train so young. Half the guards Lachlan oversaw had been sent from surrounding areas by their own parents, who knew that life at the castle was a far better fate than farming or trade. Laird Campbell took care of those in his charge like family, ensuring they had food, shelter, and clothing no matter what. It was a good life to be part of his community.

But he had not been sent for a better life. The Stewarts and the Campbells had been seeking an alliance and sending Lachlan to work as a guard for Laird Campbell had ensured loyalty. And while at first, Lachlan had missed his family terribly, he had come to love Castle Morcoille. It was his home now, and when he competed in the annual games, he competed for the praise of the laird, more so than that of his father.

As Lachlan looked to the castle's west, he saw the

beginnings of preparations for the games, which were to be held in three days. Tents were going up, under which would lay banquet tables filled with all manner of delicacies and drink. The lawn was being readied for the caber toss, hammer throw, stone put, and sheaf toss, and new archery targets were being laid nearby, giving men of the castle their yearly chance to best Lachlan and fail spectacularly at it.

Lachlan smiled at the thought of all the coin and whisky he would win as a result of the losing bets from those who still, even now, doubted his archery skills, but his thoughts were interrupted by the sight of Rowan walking across the grounds, seemingly straight toward him.

This was odd for many reasons, chief of which was that he and Rowan did not generally interact intentionally. Or rather, Rowan never spoke with him intentionally. Lachlan, of course, had been seeing her two mornings a week for over a year and would have gladly taken on a hundred more morning guard shifts if it meant the chance for more opportunities to rest his eyes upon her bonny self.

"Lachlan," Rowan said, and the sight of her in the midmorning sun struck Lachlan speechless. Her cheeks were rosy with exertion, and her hair was uncharacteristically out of its plait, falling over her shoulders and down her back. It was rare for him to have such a good look at her since their morning encounters were usually held at still dark, and he couldn't help but be stirred anew at her beauty.

I wish it were dark now, Lachlan thought, for suddenly, Rowan was not the only one with pink cheeks. Lachlan tried to compose his face into a mask of coolness, but he worried he had failed when Rowan's mouth quirked up at one side, her face transforming into a smirk he knew to mean she was inwardly laughing at his expense.

"Good day, Rowan," Lachlan said, staring off just over her shoulder, allowing his mind and body a moment to cool from the sight of her.

"I've come to tell ye there is a slight change in the schedule for the games. We're moving the archery contest to last. Can ye relay this to yer guards?" she asked.

Lachlan ought to have made some snide remark about the laird's daughter concerning herself with the minutiae of planning the games, but instead, he blurted out, "What? Why?"

The archery contest had been the first event for as long as the games had been run, which was at least thirty years. The castle had been holding them since the first year Laird Campbell took over from his own father.

"It is nae for ye to question the decisions of me or me father, Lachlan. Simply do as I say and notify the guards so ye can make the necessary alterations to yer shifts," she said haughtily, and then, before Lachlan could utter a response, she turned on her heel and strode off, her hair nearly slapping him in the face as she did so.

Lachlan ducked, and while he was crouched low to the ground, was fascinated to find that his vantage point allowed him to perfectly see the dirk that Rowan hid in the boot that, along with its mate, was beating a hasty retreat from him.

What need does a lass have for a blade on her own lands, he wondered. *Especially with me as head guard.* He would have been insulted that Rowan did not feel safe under his protection had his mind not immediately returned to the matter of the archery contest and its new and very inconvenient timing.

He had spent days working on the schedule for the guard shifts, trying to ensure that every guard had a chance to enjoy the annual games while maintaining the castle's usual level of security. The shift that coincided with the archery contest had been particularly difficult to organize since Lachlan knew that all the men would want to participate, and this meant rotating the guards around the castle after each round of the contest.

He had also arranged the schedule so that he would be near his father much of the day, either actively participating in games or passing by the man on his way to and from a guard shift. Now, Lachlan would likely only see his father for an hour at most. And with no family weddings or funerals in sight, it would be another year before he had any more time in his presence. The thought sent a pang of sadness to his chest, a pang that was quickly replaced by anger targeted directly at Rowan.

Taking off at a run, he made his way back to the castle, using the kitchen door to ascend directly up the stairs that led to the floor where he and the other high-ranking members of the castle's community slept.

Pushing his door open, he ignored the welcoming sight of his bed and its folded duvet and instead made directly for the writing desk pushed under the room's only window. Grabbing a quill, ink, and paper, he settled himself in front of the dying embers of the previous night's fire and began the tedious task of changing the schedule he had worked so hard on, cursing Rowan all the while.

He had no valid reason to believe the contest's change was her fault, but a sneaking suspicion told him that somehow, she was the reason for his misery.

No doubt she would be delighted to think so, he grumbled to himself.

6

———

"Och. 'Tis starting," Blair cried in excitement, grasping Rowan's arm as she leaned out of her seat to see the bagpipers marching across the grounds.

Rowan smiled at her friend and sat back in her chair. Though she did not show it quite as openly as Blair, she too was looking forward to the day.

The annual games held happy memories for her; they were often one of the few that she and her sisters had gotten along, too involved in the festivities to find reasons to bicker. Her father was always in a fine mood on these days as well. He had met Rowan's mother at one such annual game, and Rowan had often thought her father looked ten years younger on these days, as though he was reliving the moment he first laid eyes on the young Freya Fraser.

As the bagpipers wound down their song, Laird Campbell himself stood up and, clearing his throat, began to recite the schedule for the games. Befuddled expressions crossed a few faces as he ended his speech with the announcement of the archery contest, which was now the closing event for the day before the feast.

"Why is the archery contest last? 'Tis been first as long as I can remember," Blair said, looking at Rowan for answers.

Rowan shrugged, attempting nonchalance, but she knew that it was for naught.

Blair read her immediately, bumping Rowan's shoulders and whispering, "What plan do ye have up yer sleeve, Rowan Campbell? I ken there is one. That's yer mischievous face. I would ken it anywhere."

Dropping her mask of indifference, Rowan turned with a wicked smile to her friend and whispered, "Ye'll see soon enough."

Soon, however, was a relative term, for it was nearing late afternoon by the time the men lined up for the archery contest. They all appeared tired, and a few looked too drunk to even hold a bow properly, let alone send an arrow straight to the target's middle.

"There's nae near so much competition for victor this year," Blair commented, as though she could read Rowan's mind. "But then, I supposed that was yer plan all along."

"Indeed," Rowan smiled, for this had, of course, been the reason she had moved the contest. The annual games drew the biggest crowd of men of any event of the year and were, therefore, the most expedient way for Rowan to find a husband by her father's proposed deadline. And the archery contest would be the battleground where her potential betrothed would unwittingly fight for her hand.

Though the most important quality in a husband was, of course, that he did not attempt to subdue her, there was little practical way for Rowan to test that in a man before their wedding. So instead, she had decided that she would choose the strongest, most stubborn man, one with a natural affinity for archery, which above all else was her first love. She wanted a man who could still succeed at his chosen craft after a full day of drinking, competing, and making merry.

After all, it would have been easy enough to win the archery contest had it been held at its usual time in the morning, when energy was high, and porridge had just been eaten, giving men the strength they needed to get through the day.

It was only a truly great man who could hit the target when he was tired, cold, drunk, and hungry. That man would need inner reserves of strength to accomplish this feat, and that was the man Rowan wanted to marry. She needed someone as strong as she, as stubborn as she. They might not love each other, but they would be alike enough to understand each other. That was what she wanted. Someone who appreciated her just as she was and did not expect any more or less.

Rowan's eyes moved over the line of men in front of her now, preparing their bows and arrows, alighting on one figure whose form stood out against the waning sun.

Lachlan.

She had forgotten about Lachlan's talent for archery in all the fervor of the past few days. In fact, she had not thought of him since that morning when she had informed him of the change in schedule.

A pity, since it now dawned on her that the most likely champion of the contest was he.

He seemed as hale as he had at the beginning of

the games, his shoulders thrown back, spine straight, strong legs braced apart. He was every inch the renowned hunter and guard, exuding tenacity.

I should have spiked his ale with drams of whisky when he was nae looking, Rowan thought glumly, though, in truth, she doubted even that would have made a difference to his capabilities. It was common knowledge that Lachlan had beaten every single man in the castle and the four nearby villages at archery at one time or another, often when he was well into his cups. The very idea that anyone still tried to best him at all was rather laughable and made her once again berate herself for forgetting his reputation in the midst of all her planning.

"It will be Lachlan. I'll bet ye three of those seed cakes me mum makes that ye like so much. Lachlan will win, just as he always does," Blair said to Rowan as she took a sip of the hard apple cider in her cup.

"And what makes ye think that? He might be tired. He has been guarding on and off all day, overseeing his men and the contest, ensuring our safety. I doubt he's even had a moment to eat since breakfast," Rowan said, more to convince herself than Blair.

"Ye and I both ken a little fatigue and an empty

stomach will nae fell a man like Lachlan. He is far stronger than that," Blair said.

Rowan did not miss the sly smile her friend gave her.

Rolling her eyes like a petulant child, Rowan turned back to the contest and watched as the first man released his arrow, just barely hitting the outermost circle of the target.

Down the line the shots went, each man taking his turn. Those who hit the target dead center were invited to the next round, where they competed again, along with a few guards, who seemed to be trading shifts so that each had his turn.

It looked like a complicated system, the guards filtering in and out with the rounds, each stopping to confer with the others, as was mandatory when handing over a shift. Rowan realized then how much work she must have made for Lachlan, who had no doubt planned the guard shifts and transitions days, maybe even weeks in advance of the games.

This further complicated her feelings toward Lachlan, who was steadily advancing through the rounds until the contest was between him and a stranger with dark brown hair whom Rowan did not recognize. His clothes were fine, denoting an elevated station.

"Blair, do ye ken who that man competing against Lachlan is?" Rowan asked, learning toward Blair.

"'Tis nae very like ye to inquire after a man's identity," Blair teased, but she held off her laughter at the sight of desperation on Rowan's face.

Rowan waited without encouraging Blair's mirth.

"He's the son of a clan leader from the far north, near Skye," Blair told her. Rowan nodded, thankful that, unlike her, Blair always listened keenly to castle gossip.

"And is he... is he betrothed?" Rowan asked, barely able to get the words out, she was so nervous.

If he is, then I must marry Lachlan. He'll be me only option, she thought, and could not tell if the sudden lightheadedness she felt was from disgust or excitement, nor did she want to.

"Aye, he is," Blair said, giving Rowan a strange look. Rowan knew it was because in all the many years they had known each other, she had never inquired after a man's eligibility. "To the lass over there," Blair said, nodding her head toward a bonny blond lass near the table spread with cakes and biscuits.

Rowan nodded and turned forward, readying herself to stomach her fate.

But just as Lachlan raised his bow and prepared to shoot, a thought struck her.

He might have bested the rest of the men, but can he best me? she wondered, for surely that was the true test of a good husband, someone who not only shared her interests, her stubbornness, but could accept the idea of a woman who was stronger than he. That was the mark of a truly good mate.

7

Lachlan looked over his shoulder at Rowan, who was sitting back in her chair, her arms crossed over her chest and a self-satisfied grin on her face.

He did not have time to ponder the reasons behind her expression, for no sooner had he turned around than his opponent released his arrow, hitting the target. It seemed, to Lachlan's expert eye, as though the arrow had landed just off-center, perhaps by no more than a quarter of an inch.

Smiling to himself, he strung his bow and let loose his arrow, knowing even before it hit that it would seat itself directly in the inner circle. He smiled at the sound of wood meeting canvas, echoing in the silent grounds.

The crowd erupted in cheers behind him, shouting his name and crying, "He's won. He's won again."

That made seven years in a row that he'd won this contest, and still, the victory did not tire him, for Lachlan only had to look back to see the two men he admired most in the world, his father and Laird Campbell, grinning back at him, pride clear in their smiles.

"Well done, lad," his father called to him, and the off-duty guards rushed to Lachlan, clapping him on the back and congratulating him.

Lachlan was so caught up in the celebrations that at first, he did not notice that outside his little circle, all had quieted down suddenly, like the grass and trees settling just before the first clapping boom of a large thunderstorm.

But then, the men around him parted, and Rowan appeared before him, that same satisfied smile on her face.

"Well done indeed, Lachlan," she said, bowing her head at him. "Seven years in a row, is it not? Quite the accomplishment. It is nae wonder me father has entrusted our castle's protection to so great a marksman as yerself."

"Thank ye, Rowan," Lachlan said, confused as to

why she was so openly pleasant. It was unlike her to talk to him willingly, to make a spectacle of herself at a public event.

What is her game? he wondered.

Thankfully, he did not have to wonder long.

"Seven years ye have gone undefeated, and yet in all that time, ye have never competed against a woman. I wonder what the outcome might be if ye did."

A few of the men nearby chuckled, obviously finding humor in the idea of a woman taking up a bow and arrow.

But Lachlan was not laughing, for now, he could see Rowan's plan.

"Is that a challenge yer offering then, Rowan?" he asked, purposefully avoiding the gaze of the laird, who was staring at his daughter with open-mouthed astonishment.

"Aye, so it is," Rowan replied.

"Will one of ye be so kind as to find me a bow and arrow? Preferably with red fletching," she said, turning to the guards who still stood a few feet away from Lachlan.

Bernard was the first to snap out of the surprised stupor most of the menfolk seemed to be under and nearly tripped over himself running to find her requested weaponry.

As Rowan stood by him, preparing to shoot, Lachlan noticed her clothing, recognizing the dress as the same she had worn the night of her sister's wedding.

She had looked beautiful then, but now, with a bow at her shoulder and her face calm, poised, and ready to fight, Lachlan thought he had never seen a more ravishing creature in all his life. This Rowan, standing at his side, almost close enough to touch, was the version of her that he liked best.

Without further preamble, Rowan let her arrow fly, and the whole crowd gasped when she hit the mark.

Lachlan didn't miss Rowan's look over her shoulder at her father, no doubt gauging his reaction.

When she turned back to him, she was wearing the widest smile he had ever seen on her face.

What a shame she will nae be wearing it in a moment when I best her, he thought to himself just before he released his arrow.

It too hit center, and one of the men designated to settle any ties in the games that day took out a small ruler from his sporran and walked toward the targets. Lachlan could see the man muttering to himself as he measured the radius of each target's innermost circle, judging each arrow's distance from the dead center.

After a few minutes, the man turned back around and told the crowd, "Rowan is the winner."

Lachlan was shocked, though he supposed he shouldn't have been. After all, he had seen her practice, had seen her hit center twenty times in a row without a lick of sunshine to help her aim. She could shoot by feel, the mark of a truly skilled archer. He had just never thought her as skilled as him.

Turning toward her, he held out his hand for the customary shake between winner and loser.

However, instead of taking his hand, Rowan looked toward the crowd, staring straight at her father as she said, "I have chosen me betrothed. I will wed Lachlan Stewart one week from this day."

8

R owan delighted in the look of surprise that crossed Lachlan's face, letting it overwhelm her feelings of trepidation.

It was far more pleasant to once again see that she had beaten him in a game than to think about the fact that in a week's time, he would be her husband and she his wife. She would be tied to him forever after, living with him, sharing her life with him.

He was, after all, not the husband she had expected.

She had, in her silly naïveté, assumed that the archery champion would be a man from some far-off clan whom she had never met before and therefore had no preconceived notions of.

To know that, instead, she was marrying Lachlan, whose presence never failed to both amuse and infuriate her, was difficult to swallow.

So, she did not swallow it, continuing to stare at her betrothed as he looked from her to her father to a man off to the side of the archery grounds, which, now that Rowan took a closer look at him, bore a striking resemblance to Lachlan.

That cannae be... surely it cannae—

Her thoughts were interrupted by the man himself striding toward her and Lachlan, his face beaming.

"At last, ye've found yerself a wife. And a bonny one at that," the man cried as he wrapped Lachlan in a hug.

Lachlan patted his father on the back, looking at Rowan with yet more surprise. She did not have time to consider the ramifications of meeting her betrothed's father, however, because her own father was now striding very quickly toward her.

Pulling her to the side, away from the crowd and prying eyes and listening ears, he turned them so they faced the forest.

"Lass. Och, I cannae tell ye how happy I am," he said, scooping her up and hugging her so tightly Rowan could hear her corset creak.

She laughed, or rather, attempted to laugh, as her father set her down on the ground and placed his hands on her shoulders.

"Lachlan is the best man for a hundred miles, two hundred even. Had I had my pick of a thousand men, he would have been me choice for ye. He is good and kind, and he'll make ye the best husband ye could have hoped for. And I daresay ye'll get that love match ye were hopin' for all along."

Rowan did not know what to say to that, for she had not yet come to terms with spending the rest of her life with Lachlan, let alone loving him. So, instead of answering, she simply stood on her tiptoes and kissed her father on the cheek and smiled at him, hoping that his own happiness would shield him from the anxiety she was sure was evident on her face.

She tried to hide it when, a few minutes later, Lachlan introduced her to his father, who also hugged her, but, unlike her father, did so in a far more comfortable, less pain-inducing manner.

"'Tis a blessing to meet the lass who will finally make a husband of me Lachlan. When I sent him here all those years ago, I never imagined he'd catch the eye of the laird's daughter," he said with a full-belly laugh.

His joviality eased Rowan's nerves, and she found herself relaxing for the first time all day.

"It is a blessing to be marrying yer son, Laird Stewart. He's a fine man, and I ken..." she paused and turned to look at Lachlan, "I ken we shall have a good life together."

She had almost said, "I ken he will make me happy," but she had caught herself, remembering that relying on others to care for her gave them the power in the relationship. She had lived most of her life looking after herself, making decisions that suited her and no one else, and she did not plan to cede control to Lachlan once they had wed, no matter what tradition and custom might dictate.

As the day went on, Rowan found herself worrying more and more about whether Lachlan would let their relationship be one based on equality. She knew him. He was pig-headed and stubborn, just like her, and she had seen him flirt with enough of the pretty kitchen maids to assume that his ideal woman was a feminine lass who could sew his shirts and look after his bairns.

What if he tries to mold me into that? What if he

expects me to be a proper lass? she worried. Her father had wanted her to have a husband to *occupy* her time, and now, Rowan worried that Lachlan expected the same, expected her to dress prettily and spend her days looking after him the way a wife ought to.

But if Rowan knew one thing about herself, it was that she rarely did things the way they ought to be done by one of her gender. And after two decades of living as such, she was not sure she could change her ways even if she wanted to.

This headache-inducing thought made it impossible to enjoy the afternoon or the evening when the celebrations grew replete with all she detested—fine clothing, crowds of people, loud noises, drunk men and women, and, most horribly of all, conversations with strangers.

The reveling was raucous indeed, for now, it was not just the annual games that everyone was celebrating, but an impending wedding as well. She was assaulted by well-wishers, men coming up to tell her how well she had chosen, women telling her what a handsome man her betrothed was. The cook even came to speak to her, tears running down the older woman's face as she told Rowan how she had always dreamed of baking one last wedding cake for the laird's lasses, and how pleased she was that now she would finally have the chance to truly perfect her vanilla sponge.

Rowan did not have the heart to tell the poor woman that she preferred honey to vanilla; she doubted she would even have time to eat anything at her own wedding if today were any indication of the hectic nature of the festivities to come.

She shuddered, thinking of all the attention that day would draw to her; today alone, she had spoken to more people in one afternoon than she often did in an entire month.

Suddenly, Rowan wished her sisters were at her side, for they had all been through the process. Normally, she eschewed their advice since it generally consisted of romantic counsel, which had never before applied to her. But now, she longed for them to gather around her and tell her what to expect on that day and how to build a life with someone that she only knew from arguments and petty squabbles.

But as she looked around her, suddenly feeling desperately lonely despite the crowded room in front of her, she realized that it was not her sisters she needed, but Blair.

Her sisters would not calm her. More than likely, they would scare her with tales of the wedding night and the marriage beyond it. They would make fun of her for her naïveté, treating her like the mischievous child they still saw her as. They would tell her all the ways she was inadequate, all the things she ought to change about herself, convincing her that no matter what she did, she would never be good enough, not for them, and certainly not for Lachlan.

Blair would do the opposite. She alone would be able to appease the worries blooming like snowflakes in Rowan's mind.

But Blair and her mother had been called away hours ago to tend to a few of the men who had injured themselves during the games. It was always the way—men's hubris made them believe they were far younger and stronger than they were in truth. The injuries were minor; just a few shoulders popped out of their sockets and a strained wrist, but it had been enough to keep Blair and Mary occupied for much of the afternoon and evening.

Which meant that when Rowan finally found a corner of the hall to hide in so she could enjoy a tankard of cider, a few pieces of shortbread, and a bit of peace and quiet, there was no one to console her. No one to counsel her. She needed Blair's steadying presence more than ever, and absent her best friend and confidante, her mind continued to race, lingering on a horrible future as Lachlan's bride, stuck inside, stripped of her bow and arrow, and made to play a bonny housewife. The worries grew more acute, and Rowan found herself berating herself with such ferocity that she eventually drew her knees into her chest and tucked her head between them, taking fast, shallow breaths that brought tears to her eyes.

It was the second time she had cried in as many weeks, a rarity for her. She could feel the pieces of her very self, her soul, beginning to crumble.

What have I done? she wondered, listening to all the revelers in the hall, laughing as though they had not a care in the world. And tonight, they didn't. They were full of good food, drink, and the knowledge that the laird's errant daughter had finally found a mate. All was well with them.

Rowan, however, felt as if nothing in her world would ever be right again. She wanted to slap herself for being so naïve as to not remember that in deciding her husband using the venue of an archery contest, she was dooming herself to a life spent with Lachlan Stewart, a man who made her feel a mix of many emotions that above all left her angry and confused.

As though she herself had conjured him, someone began shouting his name to her right.

"Lachlan. Where's yer wife to be? Surely she ought to be celebrating with ye," a different voice boomed, followed by a drunken laugh.

She quickly wiped the tears from her cheeks and picked her head up, watching as Lachlan looked around, a wide, easy smile on his face as he searched the room. She felt a jolt of embarrassment the moment his eyes locked on hers, for they softened in what she could only assume was pity at the tracks of tears on her cheeks and the fetal posture of her limbs.

Rowan hated to be pitied. It implied there was something about her that was weak and tender, in need of care, a care that she herself was not strong enough to provide.

She found that she was clutching her fists, her entire body wrought with tension as she waited for Lachlan to walk over to her, to wrap his arms around her and play her doting betrothed to the menfolk around him.

It was quite a surprise when he did no such thing, instead winking at her before turning around, shrugging his shoulders and saying something that sounded like, "I cannae find her, but I suspect she is with Blair, celebrating in their way."

He was letting her remain hidden. He was merely being kind.

Kindness was something Rowan had never considered in a prospective husband, but perhaps it ought to have been at the top of her list of necessary qualities. Because with kindness came respect, and wasn't that what she had truly been looking for? Someone to respect her wishes, her way of doing things?

Perhaps being married to him will nae be so bad after all, she thought with cautious, closely guarded optimism as she settled deeper into her chair, unfurling her legs and arms out in front of her.

Reaching out to her plate of shortbread, Rowan selected the biggest piece and brought it to her mouth, letting the taste overwhelm her, until all her thoughts, worries, and machinations fled, leaving her with a modicum of peace for the first time in days.

9

———

Five days before the wedding

I *should have kenned she would nae stay away,* Lachlan thought to himself as he watched Rowan head for the armory.

It was a blisteringly cold day, and she was wrapped up warmly, with a knit grey scarf encircling her neck. Lachlan knew there were sheaves of paper containing lists of things that Rowan needed to complete before the wedding, and yet here she was, sacrificing sleep and energy to practice her archery.

Taking a deep breath, Lachlan stepped out from his usual hiding place and walked directly into Rowan's path. Her eyes were on the ground, but he assumed she would look up when she came to the door.

He was wrong.

Instead, Rowan walked directly into him. Shock flashed across her face before a different emotion took over—defensiveness.

She crouched down, her hands raised in fists, her knees bent in a position of attack.

It was to Lachlan's detriment that he chose this moment to guffaw openly, laughing at the lass as she glared at him like he was the most distasteful beast she had ever laid eyes upon.

"Lachlan. What are ye doing here, scaring me like that?" she shouted.

Lachlan had not expected her to shout—it was, after all, not even sunrise yet, and most people in the five-mile radius were asleep in their beds—but he reacted quickly, roughly grabbing her arm and pulling her into the quiet of the armory, where the thick interior walls would, he hoped, block out any more infuriated screeching she might choose to do.

"Guarding the castle, as I ought to be. What are ye doing here?" he countered, crossing his arms and leering over her.

"Yer not me keeper, and 'tis none of yer business what I do with my time, so I'll thank ye to get out of me way," she said, trying to wrench her arm from his grip. She failed, and Lachlan pulled her further into the armory until they were standing below an unlit torch near a section of wall containing a fearsome array of axes.

"I'm afraid I cannae let ye. Ye need to get yerself back to bed, where a bride five days out from her wedding with more to do than God himself should be," he told her, releasing her arm so he could retrieve a spark from another torch and light the torch above them. When the flame caught, and the light shone down, it revealed Rowan's expression, which looked murderous.

"Listen closely, Lachlan Stewart, for I shall nae say this twice," Rowan said, her voice dropping to a menacing whisper as she stepped toward him, invading his space with her sweet honey scent. "Ye donnae tell me what to do. Not now, when we're betrothed, and not in five days' time when we're wed. I'm me own woman, I make me own choices, and I intend to continue in this manner for the rest of my days. Ye will nae have a say in me life, and I will nae have a say in yers," she told him.

She was glaring at him, and Lachlan knew that she was trying to intimidate him, as was her habit. It was his usual tendency to retort with something insulting and witty, but instead of doing so, he could not help but notice how bonny her eyes were.

Dark sable eyelashes lined the almond shape of her upper and lower lids. Her irises were so dark as to almost appear black in the relative dimness, but when he leaned toward her, the light from the torch above them revealed flecks of amber and gold scattered around her pupil like rays of the sun.

Lachlan also noted that her irises were rimmed in regal purple, and he could not help but laugh at this, for in another life, Rowan surely would have been a queen, ruling her people with a fair but commanding fist and making even the most formidable of opponents shake in their boots.

"Do ye really think laughing at me again will endear ye to me, dear husband-to-be?" she said, her tone laced with sardonic spite.

Lachlan quieted at that, stifling his chuckles and purposefully turning his mouth down, hiding the mirth that was still bubbling in him. The more ferocious she appeared, the more the desire to laugh rose in him. It was a rather inconvenient correlation.

"Did ye hear what I said?" Rowan asked, still looking thunderous.

"Aye, lass. I will nae laugh at ye again. Ye have my

most sincere apologies," Lachlan said, dipping his chin to make a show of being suitably cowed.

Rowan huffed a loud exhale and rolled her eyes.

"Nae, before. What I said about how I want to treat me when we are..." she seemed to struggle for a moment, and Lachlan understood why when he heard her next words. "When we are husband and wife."

It had taken him little time to accept his fate; after all, it was what he always had secretly wished would happen. To live out a fantasy was true bliss indeed, even if the fantasy included a woman with emotions more turbulent than the waves of the nearby loch.

Rowan's brow furrowed as she spoke, her voice losing some of the combative tone that had colored it only moments ago. Her lips were turned down, but even in that expression, they were still the most perfect he had ever seen, making him think of that line from Romeo and Juliet. About lips standing like blushing pilgrims, ready to make things better with a kiss.

But if there was one thing Lachlan knew about Rowan Campbell, it was that she was most certainly not a lass who could be mollified by the meeting of lips.

At least nae yet, he reminded himself, for perhaps, in time, in their marriage, she might change and come to see that often a kiss was just what was needed to dissolve the tension between a man and his woman.

Sighing, he nodded and took a step backward, away from Rowan and her bewitching eyes and lips.

"Aye, lass, I heard ye. And I donnae plan to change yer whole way of living. I was only saying that perhaps today, mere days before our wedding, ye might put down the bow and arrow and get yerself some rest so that ye can attend to those duties expected of ye as a bride."

"Bow and arrow? How did ye...?" she asked, trailing off as her gaze seemed to lose focus, her mind clearly deep in thought, perhaps trying to understand how Lachlan might have discovered her secret.

She began to gnaw her lower lip again, a sight that normally would have had Lachlan's full attention, but his senses were suddenly alert to the sound of soft footsteps outside.

Years as a guard had honed his senses until he could detect the subtlest change in his environment, and those footsteps were enough to raise the hairs on the back of his neck, for it meant an intruder was near.

He knew this because there was only one kind of person out and about this early in the morning—excepting Rowan—and that was the castle guards. And the footsteps could not belong to one of them, for there had been no call.

Years ago, the lead guard before him had taught all the men how to imitate the call of the chaffinch in order to alert the guard on duty of his colleague nearby.

Ears trained on the noise outside, his body ready for a fight, Lachlan found himself momentarily distracted by Rowan, who was preparing to open her lips and speak, most likely in a loud and brash manner that would make their presence immediately known, more so than the lone flickering light above them, an odd sight in a normally abandoned section of the grounds at this time of day.

Rushing toward her, Lachlan clapped a hand over Rowan's mouth and spun her so that her back was pressed to his front, her ear just a breath away from his mouth.

"Dinnae say a word, lass. There is someone outside, and our safety depends on being quiet as mice in the night, ye ken?" he whispered, his lips nearly brushing against her ear as he rasped.

Rowan nodded, her head moving softly against his chest, and Lachlan dropped his hand from her mouth, deliberately avoiding the realization that her lips had touched his hand and his had touched her hair. The situation was dire, but he could not help relishing the closeness, the chance to be in her vicinity and breathe her scent in—sweet clove honey and a mixture of wood smoke and dew. It was intoxicating.

Lachlan heard Rowan inhale a sharp breath as the footsteps grew closer. He could feel the muscles in her arms and back tense, as though she too was preparing to attack, but that would not be necessary.

I will protect her, nae matter what happens. It was what he had been doing for years already.

10

Rowan watched as a figure came into the doorway, their identity shielded due to the shadows occupying all but the small space afforded by the torch above their heads.

"Who are ye, and what is yer business here before dawn?" Lachlan barked to the figure, his voice strong and clear in the otherwise silent armory. She was surprised at how commanding he sounded. Indeed, she was surprised about much at the moment. That she had let Lachlan silence her with his hand, that she had let him pull her close for protection. That she had even followed him into the armory in the first place.

Why am I obeying him? Why am I letting him be in

control? she asked herself, but instead of answers, her mind gave her only more questions, one of which chilled her to her core and ignited a fire in her belly, unlike anything that whiskey or ale could ever produce— *Why am I enjoying it?*

She was kept from more postulation as the person in front of them took one, then two, then three steps forward, bringing them into the triangle of light the torch cast.

It was a lad no older ten years of age. He took one look at the formidable figure Lachlan cut, then turned and ran.

Lachlan immediately dropped his arms from around Rowan and sprinted out of the armory to follow the lad.

Rowan was fast on his heels, shouting, "Wait. Stop running, both of ye."

She had recognized the lad immediately from his hair, so blond it was nearly white. He was one of the new stable boys, hired to help care for the horses of the many visitors who would arrive today and tomorrow to attend the wedding festivities. He was also a cousin of Ainslee's, and the maid had introduced them when Rowan left for a walk to the MacManuss the day before and happened to pass by the stables and see Ainslee talking to the lad.

Summoning all her strength, Rowan sprinted and came to a stop in front of Lachlan. A part of her had hoped he would crash into her—both because it was only fair after what he had done to her only a quarter of an hour ago and because she already missed the warmth of him so close to her—but his quick reflexes allowed him to halt just before he ran her down.

"What do ye think yer doing? The lad is getting away," he said, trying to brush past her. Rowan spread her arms out to block him.

"He's nae a criminal, Lachlan. He's a stable boy and Ainslee's cousin. I ken him. He does not mean to harm us, and I'll thank ye not to scare a decade off his lifespan by chasing him all around the castle grounds before the cocks have even crowed."

Lachlan rolled his eyes but acquiesced, and Rowan lowered her arms and turned to find the lad, whose name was Logan, cowering in his boots.

"I was nae trying to scare ye," he said, the terror quaking his voice, only growing stronger as Lachlan slowly walked toward him. "I could nae sleep, and I wanted a walk. I'm verra sorry for causing ye distress," he said, sniffing, clearly trying not to cry as he looked away, pointedly avoiding Lachlan's gaze.

"'Tis fine, Logan. We ken ye did nae mean to hurt

us. Ye merely surprised us. This early in the morning, there are usually few about the grounds. Why were ye out at this time of day?" Rowan asked, softening her voice as she stepped toward him and placed what she hoped was a comforting hand on his shoulder.

Logan was silent, and Rowan looked over her shoulder to find Lachlan glaring at the lad. Rowan glowered in return and mouthed, 'Be kind,' before bringing her attention back to Logan.

"Go on, lad, tell us," she said, speaking to him as she would a newborn lamb.

"I could nae sleep. I was too excited about the wedding and all the horses coming today. Anders says there might be Caspian horses," he said, animation replacing some of the fear in his eyes.

Rowan felt herself soften even further, for it was clear from the way the lad spoke that horses were his passion. She could well relate to that. This morning she had woken up earlier than usual, heeding the call of her bow and arrows that begged her to get down and practice, to clear her mind and hone her craft.

She was also pleased to know that Anders, the Dutchman who oversaw the stables, had finally found a stable boy who shared his interest in specialty horse breeds, of which Caspians were one.

I will have to send him a message later, asking for the lad to be given a permanent position after the wedding, she thought. It would be good for Ainslee to have more family close by, and the stables could use another equestrian enthusiast.

"I ken what it is like to lose sleep over an impending celebration, but I will tell the local healer to make ye a tincture to help ye sleep. Ye will need yer energy to keep after all those new and exotic animals," she said, squeezing his shoulder before releasing it and bidding him go back to bed.

The lad did so with renewed vigor, practically skipping to the back entrance of the castle that led to the servants' quarters.

She watched him go, a small smile on her face.

Until Lachlan opened his mouth.

"That was foolish of ye," he said from behind her, his words laced with derision. Any warm feelings Rowan might have cultivated for him vanished in that instant.

"Why must you ruin everything?" she muttered.

She had been glad that he allowed her to handle things with Logan, interpreting it as a gesture of faith in her strength and ability to navigate what had, at first, seemed a dangerous situation. But she had been mistaken. And Rowan hated to be mistaken.

Lachlan ran a hand down his face, revealing an expression at once infuriated and fatigued. "Ruin everything? Is that really what ye think? Och, Rowan, are we really to carry on in our marriage exactly as we have, bickering like children? Will naught change?"

Rowan turned to him and opened her mouth.

He did not give her time to answer, continuing with his rant and growing more agitated by the word. "Is this a foreshadowing of our marriage? I try to protect ye, to care for ye, and rather than show me gratitude, ye treat me with contempt?"

"Protect me? Care for me? Did I nae made meself clear when I said I would nae need, nor want, yer help in those areas?" Rowan growled at him, though her anger was aimed almost entirely at herself, for relishing the feeling of being enveloped in his arms, ceding control to him and relying on his strong, able body and quick mind to keep her from harm.

I hate him, Rowan thought, but she immediately knew the falsehood of that statement. She did not, could not hate Lachlan, but she loathed the turbulence he caused in her head and heart as they struggled to understand the mess of feelings he brought up in her.

"Aye, ye did. But ye have to understand that at that moment, I reacted on instinct. Me mind told me to look out for ye because that is what I have been trained to do, that is what I have done for so long," he said, and Rowan did not miss the hint of emotion in those last words.

But instead of relenting, showing him mercy and understanding, she said, "Your instinct should be to obey me as the laird's daughter. I told ye how I wanted to be treated, and ye did nae listen," her words so cold they sent shivers down her own back.

It was as though she were looking at herself as an observer, seeing her treating her betrothed like a shrew would, but unable to stop because to stop meant bending to feelings she didn't understand and showing a side of herself that even she was not familiar with.

"And yet ye ken that I will nae treat ye as such because I am to be yer husband, and in times such as when an unknown stranger approaches us, it will always be me instinct to look after ye. I cannae change that about meself, Rowan, nae do I want to. And ye kenned that when ye chose a guard for yer husband. So I must ask, why did ye choose me if ye kenned what I was like?"

She remained silent.

Running a hand over his beard, he asked again, "Why did ye choose me when there are hundreds of men ye could pick from? Why me? Please tell me, for I have been trying to reason it out for days, and I cannae understand it."

Rowan opened her mouth, but despite the many possible answers that came to mind, none of them was right. She might have chosen him because he was the victor of the archery contest, but as to why she kept him, she could not explain.

She looked past him toward the practice grounds, wishing that she could run for them and shoot arrow after arrow until her mind was empty and her hands were calloused. She did not want to stand here discussing marriage or emotions. She wanted, more than anything at that moment, to be alone, away from Lachlan and everything he made her feel and think.

'Tis too much. He's too much, she thought, squeezing her eyes shut and hoping he would be

gone when she opened them. It was a tactic she had used as a child when her sisters got on her nerves. It had not worked then, and it did not work now.

When she cracked one lid open, there was Lachlan towering over her, his expression a mixture of anger and unguarded yearning.

It made her stomach drop, and the breath leave her lungs.

"I... I cannae explain it," she said, shaking her head. "I'm sorry, Lachlan, but I cannae."

Lachlan nodded, appearing resigned, and began to walk away from her toward the castle.

Rowan followed him, not knowing what to say and yet suddenly not wanting him to leave, not when they both seemed so despondent.

Suddenly, he turned around, so quickly that she barely had time to halt before he was in front of her, his chest just inches away from hers, his breaths coming fast and short, making small clouds of air that immediately evaporated into the chill that she could suddenly feel right down to her bones.

"Today is not the only day I've gone against yer wishes, lass. I've been protecting ye for ye for years. And do ye ken why?" Lachlan asked, his voice lowering, growing hoarse with feeling.

"Protecting me? How? When?" she asked, confused. What had either of them ever done for one another but throw insults and make jokes at the other's expense?

"I ken ye practice archery in the morning twice a week. That's how I found ye today. I saw ye the first time ye ever took up a bow and arrow, and the next day, I switched my guard shifts so that I would be there each morning ye rose early to walk down the practice grounds. I wanted to be sure ye were safe and that nae one found out about yer affinity with the bow. I've watched over ye for two years, and I have said nae a word to anyone because I kenned how important it was to ye to have that time to yerself."

"Ye've been watching me?" Rowan whispered, feeling violated.

She had crept out of the castle for weeks to learn the schedule of the guard shifts and how best to sneak out to the armory. She had known, instinctively, that while her father might tolerate her interest in healing, he would not feel the same about his daughter taking up a weapon normally meant solely for men. And in all that time watching the guards, she had never, not once, seen Lachlan.

"I never noticed ye. How is that possible?"

A grin crossed his face. "I am head guard for a reason, lass. I can be as quiet as a mouse and just as invisible when I like. When ye let loose that first arrow, yer smile was the most beautiful thing I have ever seen. A private sunrise only for me," he said, his eyes dipping to her lips and lingering for a moment. "I kenned how happy archery made ye, and I dinnae want that ruined by some castle guard finding ye in the early dawn hours and telling the laird. So I have stood out in the cold for two years, making sure that ye had those hours to do what ye loved, unimpeded by anyone, friend or foe."

Lachlan was looking at her with true affection.

Rowan knew because it was the same look that Kirsten had given Robert the day of their wedding.

"I did that because," Lachlan started, pausing and running his hand over his beard again, clearly nervous. Rowan found herself wondering what it would feel like under her hands. She imagined it was soft like goose down.

When Lachlan did not continue speaking, she looked up, shaking away her reverie, suddenly incredibly eager and incredibly afraid to hear the end of his sentence.

"Because I care for ye," he whispered with reverence. "Because I love ye. I have loved ye for years, lass. I have loved ye so long that I donnae ken what it is not to love ye," he said, his green eyes darkening to a glowing emerald that froze Rowan's entire body with its intensity.

"But... but..." she stuttered, furrowing her brow in frustration at her lack of coherent response. "Before last week, I dinnae even think ye enjoyed being in me presence. All we did was insult each other."

"Nay, lass. Those were not insults. They were jests. I was trying to be yer friend, to become someone ye wanted to be near. I kenned ye would nae tolerate kind words from me, that ye would assume they were flirtations and turn the other way, so I thought I might win yer friendship with humor," he said, and as he did, Rowan realized that Lachlan had indeed treated her no differently than his friends in the castle and village, with whom he was always joking.

She knew he was right in thinking she would never have trusted him if he exchanged pretty words with her. But he was wrong in thinking that she would trust him otherwise. Except for Blair and Mary MacManus, Rowan had never trusted another person in all her life, not even her father. She was not sure she was even capable.

But maybe I could trust him. He kens me, kens what I'm like, she thought, nearly emitting a bitter laugh at the irony of attaching herself to a man who, only a month ago, would have been the last of her choices for a husband, but had turned out to be exactly what she wanted and needed in a partner—someone who knew her, respected her.

And I have been horrible to him from the first.

"Why did ye continue pursuing me, even when I was so awful to ye? Even when I took yer jests for barbs? Why would ye want to be around such a shrew?" she asked.

He huffed out a breath, a faint blush creeping over his cheeks as his eyes met hers for the first time in minutes.

"Because I love ye. It is simple. And I would rather be insulted by ye and still be in yer presence than exchange pretty words with anyone else."

He loves me.

Rowan could not comprehend it. She had never thought to be loved by a man, not because she did not think herself worthy, but because she had made very clear to all the men in her locality that she was not interested in their affections.

As she gazed into Lachlan's eyes, she recognized the same look of love and adoration she had seen on Kirsten and Robert's faces the day of their wedding.

She had dismissed love as silly and meaningless, but now that she was in the glow of it, she understood what Kirsten had told her the night before she wed Robert. "To be in love is to be completely overcome. It knocks ye to the knees, breaks down yer walls until all ye can do is surrender."

Rowan found her cheeks flushing to match Lachlan's, and a deep warmth spread throughout her chest. It was his love's effect on her, and she relished it, but before it could consume her, it was cut off at the knees by a harrowing thought.

Can I ever love him back?

As though he could read her mind, Lachlan said, "Lass, do ye think ye can ever love me in return?"

Rowan understood that what he really wanted to know was whether their marriage would ever be one of romance rather than convenience. But she did not know how to answer this.

Lachlan stirred complicated feelings in her, aye, but were they romantic in nature? Was warmth in the belly, gratitude for protection, the stuff of romance? She could not say.

And so she looked at Lachlan, whom she could

see was bracing himself, and said the only thing she could. "I am sorry, but I donnae ken."

Rowan did not miss the way Lachlan's shoulders slumped in defeat, but that was all she saw, for it was with her next breath that she was turning away, her fast walk quickly turning into a run; she was eager to get as far him as possible.

He makes me feel too much, and I donnae like it.

Five Days Later

Lachlan had been pished many times in his life, and he had nearly always regretted it the next morning when the headache set in.

Now, he was sober as he had ever been and wished desperately that he were not. A headache would have muddled his mind just enough to quiet the worries that had plagued him for the last few days.

Worries, primarily, of the state of his relationship with his future wife, who had admitted she did not love him now and possibly never would.

In the days since their conversation at the

armory, Lachlan had cursed himself countless times for admitting his feelings to Rowan. He had displayed weakness, which he knew she hated. He had brought up affection, which she rarely showed. And worst of all, he had confessed love, which scared her, so much so that since then, she had avoided him as much as possible, a true feat considering how often they had been thrown together while attending various and sundry dinners and meetings in preparation for the wedding. She had spoken to him only when absolutely essential, and then, her eyes had been downcast, her mouth muttering only the most necessary words to get her point across or answer a question. If Lachlan weren't so despondent, he would have been impressed with her commitment to ignoring his existence.

But he was despondent, and more so today than all the days before, because today he was wedding a lass that was not speaking to him, did not love him, and might never forgive him for admitting that she was the person he most wanted to talk to, the woman he treasured with all his heart and soul.

Knowing he could not drown his sorrows in whiskey this early, and feeling his body resist sleep despite the comfort and warmth of his bed, Lachlan threw off his covers and was walking toward the small window in his room, hoping that the sight of the impending sunrise might brighten his spirits. He was just opening the curtains when a knock sounded at the door.

It could be her. Och, but he hoped it was. Even silent and brooding, she was still the most bonny thing he had ever seen, and to have her close enough to touch was reason enough to hastily make his bed and throw on a clean linen shirt.

But when he opened the door, it was not Rowan on the other side, but Blair, her best friend.

"Blair? What're ye doing here at the castle this early? And standing in me doorway?" he asked, bemused.

They had exchanged only a few words in the many years they had seen each other around the keep, and Lachlan could find no reason for her to be standing before him now, today of all days.

Unless...

"Is this about Rowan?" he hedged.

Blair nodded, her expression unreadable as she asked, "May I come in for a moment?"

Lachlan opened the door wider and gestured for her to make her way to the hearth. Shutting the door behind her, he strode to the fireplace and poked at the embers until they gave off enough heat to satisfy.

He sat down in the chair opposite Blair, noticing the stiff posture of her back and shoulders and the slight frown on her face.

Though he knew her but little, he had always sensed that Blair was a gentle woman, kind and thoughtful, but also quiet. She was, in many ways, the exact opposite of Rowan, and more than once, Lachlan had found himself wondering what had drawn them together as friends and kept them so close.

Blair twisted her fingers in her lap, betraying her anxiety, but she did not speak until an uncomfortable few minutes of silence passed between them, thickening the air with every tense exhale.

Finally, she said, "I've come here to give ye some advice. I ken it is nae me place, but these are extraordinary circumstances."

"Och. Are they?" Lachlan asked, unsure to what she was referring.

"Aye. Rowan will be yer wife by night's end, a fate she never contemplated until a few weeks ago. And ye are marrying the laird's daughter, an outcome I reckon ye dinnae imagine for yerself. Those sound quite extraordinary to me."

I imagined it every day, he thought but did not say.

Instead, he asked, "If it were a fate she never contemplated, why did she choose me? She certainly does nae seem happy about her choice, and as the laird's daughter, she could have cast me aside and chosen another. But she did nae. Why?"

He was hoping that Blair could give a better answer to the question that Rowan had.

Blair shrugged, some of the tension in her shoulders loosening as she replied, "Because she had to choose a husband, and because ye passed her test, out of all the men present at the annual games."

"A test?" Lachlan asked.

"Aye. And ye passed it, and in doing so, ye showed that ye could treat her like an equal. That is what she prizes most in marriage and a husband. She wants someone who will recognize her strength and ability and accept it as a part of her, rather than something strange and unladylike, something to be done away with the moment yer wed."

"So she told me," Lachlan muttered to himself.

Her face grimaced in sympathy for him, almost as though she could see the wounds in his soul. "There is something ye must understand about yer future wife, Lachlan."

"And what is that?"

"Rowan is strong, aye, but she is not absent fear."

"Fear? What could Rowan Campbell possibly have to be afeared of?" Lachlan asked with a disbelieving laugh.

"Love," Blair said.

Lachlan swallowed his chuckle, struck still by Blair's tone, which spoke of sincere concern.

"She is afraid of love?"

"Aye. Frightened it will make her vulnerable and weak, will turn her into the exact opposite of herself."

Though it pained Lachlan to hear it, he could understand Rowan's reasoning. Love was a terrifying emotion, one that shattered you from the inside out. At first, he had been consumed by his love for her, and at times, such as now, he had indeed felt weakened by it. But he had also knew there was a reason it was the most common theme in fiction and poetry —it was the fiercest emotion of them all. Greater than fear, deeper than hate, more torturous than pain. Love had made him a better man. Loving Rowan had transformed him utterly.

He smiled, remembering this. For in the last few days, he had let Rowan's fears become his own. He had felt weak and simple, hating himself for letting him giving Rowan a part of himself he thought her unable to accept.

She is nae unable, just unused to it, he realized, and some of the wounds of the last few days began to heal, allowing him to relax into his chair and smile at Blair. The first smile he had given anyone in almost a week.

"But just because she is afraid does nae mean she is incapable," Blair said, perhaps seeing the worry in his eyes. "And if there is anyone on God's earth that Rowan could fall in love with, I believe it is ye," her voice soft even as her pale grey eyes stared at him with conviction.

God, but I hope she is right, Lachlan thought, wishing he was a praying man, that he might send a plea up to the heavens above.

"Why are ye telling me this? Would Rowan nae be mad that yer spilling her secrets to a man she clearly does nae trust?" he asked.

"She is afraid to trust ye, Lachlan. Just as she is afraid to love ye. But ye cannae let her sulk in that fear. And ye cannae continue to sit here in silence, remonstrating yerself for caring for her. It does nae do either of ye any good."

"I have nae been silent. She has," Lachlan said, hearing the childish tone to his voice and immediately regretting his words.

But Rowan only laughed softly to herself and

shook her head. "I ken Rowan has been keeping her words few and far between around ye, but ye must push her. Else ye will continue in this circle of stupidity until yer marriage is ruined and ye both are miserable as two dogs caught in the rain. Ye must go to her, today, and ye must nae leave until ye have sorted out this tension between ye. Ye cannae be acting so on yer wedding day, a day that is meant to be merry for both of ye."

Lachlan nodded, knowing that Blair was correct. He ought to have gone to Rowan days ago, but after the way she had run from him, he had let his bruised pride cloud his judgment.

"Aye, I will do."

"Excellent." Blair smiled, standing up and ushering for him to do the same. "We shall go see her now."

"Now?" Lachlan sputtered.

He needed time to plan what to say, to collect his thoughts into some semblance of order, but Blair was already advancing toward the door, as though she expected him to follow her without question.

And to his surprise, he did.

12
———

Rowan was endeavoring to read a book when the knock came at her door. Tossing the book aside—her lack of attention meant she had been on the same page for a quarter of an hour now—she ran to the door and swung it open, hoping dearly it was Blair, back from the kitchen with shortbread.

She had barely been able to eat anything at dinner the night before, so addled she was by Lachlan's presence at her side. Her father had requested the "two lovebirds" be seated next to each other, and it had resulted in the most awkward meal in recent memory.

The cook had made all her favorites—leg of lamb, roasted potatoes, gravy so thick you could stand a spoon in it, and more beer bread than she had thought the ovens could handle. And because of Lachlan, she had eaten barely a bite of it.

Now, she was starving and had begged Blair to sneak into the kitchen and beg some shortbread off of Cook, who she knew would cede Rowan's every command today because it was her "special day."

It was indeed Blair at the door, and Rowan relaxed against the doorframe and smiled. "Thank God yer back. I have nae been able to concentrate, I'm so hungry," she said, smiling—

Until she looked behind Blair and saw the imposing figure of Lachlan.

"What is he doing here?" she asked Blair, but her friend ignored her and walked into the room, with Lachlan following behind.

"Did I say that ye could come into me private chambers?" Rowan asked, keeping her voice low.

Though they were to be wed that day, they were not allowed to be in a room together alone until after the ceremony. Were they caught, rumors would spread throughout the castle, and Rowan could not take any more prying eyes on her today than would already be in attendance.

"Hush, Rowan. I invited him in," Blair said,

turning around and looking at Rowan like she was a child rather than a woman and her best friend.

"And why did ye—" she began.

Blair halted her with a stay of her raised hand.

"Ye both need to talk. I will stand down the hall to ensure Ainslee does not come in and I will be back in one hour. I expect that by then, the two of ye will be the picture of marital happiness," Blair said, not waiting for their response before she walked through the door and shut it behind her, leaving Rowan alone in her room, with a man, for the first time in her life.

She glared at Lachlan, frustrated not only that he had appeared before her but that the shortbread had not.

Holding up his hands, he explained, "In my defense, Blair can be very persuasive when she wants to be."

"Aye, I ken," Rowan said, rolling her eyes and sitting on a small settee near the fire. She rested her elbows on her knees and allowed her chin to fall into her hands, not caring if she looked hunchbacked and ogre-like to Lachlan.

She was, however, suddenly rather glad she had gotten dressed and plaited her hair.

"But I am glad she persuaded me to come,

because we have much to discuss before today's events," Lachlan said, remaining standing but walking closer toward her until he was within reaching distance.

Nae that I want to reach for him, she reminded herself, even as the thought of taking his hand in hers suddenly overwhelmed every other rational impulse in her body.

"Rowan?"

She realized that while she had imagined the warmth of his palm pressed to hers, the intimacy of their fingers entwined together, Lachlan had been speaking.

"I'm sorry," she said. "I have nae been sleeping well, and it has affected my attention." It was not technically a lie; since that day at the armory, she had barely found any uninterrupted rest. All her dreams were of Lachlan, and she awakened from them confused, angry, but most of all, missing him.

Yet she was not about to show that to him, so after apologizing, she continued in her carefully casual posture, a slight glare in her eyes covering the fact that she continued to rake her eyes over his hands, which seemed to beg her to touch them, caress them, learn their every crease and callous.

"I said that I am sorry for not coming to talk to ye sooner. I ought to have, but I—"

"But ye were worried that I would bite yer head off like a fire-breathing dragon and make ye rue the day ye ever bared yer soul to me?" she asked, letting some of her embarrassment show.

For she had been ashamed, wholly disgusted in fact, by her actions. Lachlan had told her he loved her, had wanted to be her friend, and rather than giving him the respect that he and his admission deserved, she had fled, and in doing so, disrespected them both. If they were ever to have an equitable marriage, she knew she had to treat him as she would want to be treated, and there were few things she hated more than someone walking away from her in the middle of a discussion.

"Aye," he said with a laugh. "I was hurt and allowed cowardice to overtake my better instincts. I'm sorry, lass."

"Donnae apologize. I—"

Lachlan held up a hand. "Let me finish, Ro," he said, his tone beseeching.

Rowan blushed at the use of her nickname. It was one her mother had first called her, which had later been adopted by her father and Blair, and to hear it come from Lachlan's lips made her feel that much closer to him.

Nodding, she gestured for him to speak, a fluttering in her belly making her wish her stomach were filled with more than air and a craving for biscuits.

"I should have come to ye because though this was our first argument as a united pair, it will nae be the last. And we must learn to talk through strife rather than ignoring it, for in refusing to meet the problem, we make life far harder for ourselves."

Rowan nodded, knowing the truth of his words and realizing for the first time just how wise Lachlan was.

What other qualities of his have I been so blind to? she wondered.

"I apologize for scaring ye with me feelings. It was nae the right time to tell ye I love ye, but I was overcome," he explained, casting his eyes down as if temporarily reliving the moment.

Rowan felt the now-familiar heat spread through her at those three perfect words. She adored them and hated them in equal measure for how they made her feel, warm and weak all at once.

"But I will nae put pressure on ye to love me in return, now or ever. This is not a marriage as most would have it. We came together because I won a test—"

"How did ye ken about that?" Rowan asked, looking up at Lachlan, who frowned sheepishly.

"Blair. She said I passed some test ye had for me, and that is why ye chose me."

Rowan laughed. "It was not the contest. The archery contest. I told meself that a man who could win the contest and not only stand for my besting him, but also treat me like any other opponent at the end, would be me husband. And ye did," she said, smiling. "Ye treated me like I was another man."

Lachlan smiled as well, though his was tinged with disbelief. "Ye chose the person to spend the rest of yer days with from a silly contest? What if I dinnae win, and ye were stuck with some bampot?"

"I dinnae ken ye would win. I was so fixed on finding a husband that I dinnae even remember that ye were the reigning champion of the contest and have been so for as long as I can remember."

At this, Lachlan deflated somewhat. "Aye. So ye dinnae have me in mind. It could have been anyone."

Rowan reached out then and took Lachlan's hand, finding that it was even more delicious to feel his skin against hers than she could have possibly imagined.

Pulling him toward her, she looked up at him and said, "I dinnae have ye in mind, but I am dearly glad ye won. Because it is clear to me now, Lachlan Stewart, that I have done naught but underestimate ye these past years. Ye are the kindest, most clever, fiercest man I have ever met, and I am honored that today ye will become me husband."

13

____

Rowan's words were balm to Lachlan's soul, and he could not help but kneel down before her and bring her hand to his lips.

He placed a chaste kiss on her hand, and then he looked into Rowan's eyes, her eyelashes lowered as she gazed at him with more feeling than he had ever seen in her.

"Thank ye, lass. I am honored to have ye as me wife, and I promise to let ye run free and do as ye please. I love ye for yer wild spirit and free mind and would nae dare to change that about ye."

Seeing Rowan's reaction was like watching a flower unfurl in the sun. First, she picked her head up, her eyes widening, their color growing brighter and wrinkling at the corners as her lips rose in a smile. That smile brought color to her previously pallid cheeks, turning them to rosy apples. Dimples appeared at the corners of her mouth, and though Lachlan thought this every time he saw her, at this moment, he knew it was true—she had never looked more beautiful.

Of course, he ate his words hours later when she appeared down the aisle of the kirk, dressed in a gown that matched the color of the crocuses just starting to make their appearance outside.

14

––––––

Rowan's last act as an unmarried woman had been to convince her father not to order her and Lachlan a carriage to convey them to the site of their honeymoon in Inverness.

"We will ride on horseback, Father, and sleep out of doors as and when needed," she had told him, and he had easily relented, so pleased that she was getting wed, and to Lachlan no less, that he likely would have granted a thousand more outlandish favors if asked.

Now, however, Rowan was starting to wish that she had not been so fervent in her dismissal of the carriage, for Scotland had, as it was wont to do, been pouring buckets of rain on them for the better part of the day.

She had wanted to stop and camp midday to wait out the wetness, but since she was no longer the only person she had to concern herself with, she had turned to Lachlan to seek his opinion, only to be met with the sight of him tipping his head up to the sky, not seeming to care a whit that he was soaked to the bone, his hair plastered to his face.

"Och, do ye nae love a springtime rain, lass?" he had over the din of drops.

No turning back, then, she had thought ruefully.

That had been hours ago, and she had made it this far mostly by watching Lachlan delight in the weather, smiling at his childish enthusiasm for the rain that seemed unrelenting.

But now, the enjoyment was starting to wear off. She was thoroughly exhausted and in desperate need of a very long night's sleep and a warm, hearty meal. They had ridden through the night before, so excited by the wedding and their new life that sleep had seemed an inconvenience. However, she had not slept the night before that—she had not slept through the night since their conversation at the armory—and a week without proper rest and a wedding day spent walking around in uncomfortable shoes with a corset restraining her breath, which she spent mostly on conversations with people she barely knew, was now beginning to catch up with her. It was all she could do to stay sitting upright on her horse and not keel over and fall to the wet, muddy ground.

Up ahead, Lachlan turned back to check on her, and Rowan saw his smile falter when he saw her drooping shoulders and half-closed lids.

"Shall we make camp early, lass?" he asked, pointing to a copse of trees ahead.

Rowan smiled, and right then, she could have kissed her husband in gratitude.

The thought sent much-needed heat to her bones, but it also scared her. They had spent little time in close proximity to each other since the morning of their wedding when Lachlan had placed that achingly gentle yet stirring kiss to her hand, which he held as though it were the world's most precious jewel.

Immediately after that, Rowan had been whisked away by Blair and Ainslee to prepare for the day, and Lachlan had returned to his rooms, and she had not seen him until the ceremony, where they were separated by a foot of space as they read their vows. The rest of the day was even more hectic than

Rowan had feared, and though she was sat next to Lachlan for much of the night as the celebrations raged around them, they had barely spoken, let alone touched.

"Lass?" Lachlan called, and Rowan looked up to realize that her thoughts had so consumed her that she was stalled in place, her horse stomping her feet impatiently.

"I'm coming," Rowan responded, flicking the reins and, in doing so, casting off thoughts of a kiss or touch of the hands. Her horse acquiesced, and they made their way forward toward Lachlan.

He led them to a spot deep in the pine forest where the tree cover was dense enough that they were mostly sheltered from the rain. After making a fire and settling her in front of it, Lachlan began to unpack the supplies for a tent and blankets, as well as an early supper.

"When I said we ought to respect each other's wishes, I dinnae mean at the expense of our own comfort," he joked as he took some of their bags from her. "I ken I might love the rain more than most Scotsmen, but ye donnae need to bear it for me sake, Rowan. Ye ought to have told me how tired ye were," he said, shaking his head and giving her a scolding glare whose power was somewhat diminished by the wide smile on his face. Taking a loaf of bread out of one of the bags, he tore off a large piece and handed it to her.

"Eat this," he commanded, and once again, to her surprise, Rowan obeyed him without complaint.

She took the bread gratefully and ate it in two bites, not caring if her manners were not those befitting someone of her station. She was starving, and the bread was like manna from heaven.

Lachlan silently handed her another large piece, then set aside the empty bags and began to assemble their tents.

Or rather, the lone tent.

Rowan had assumed they would each have their own and had been looking forward to crawling into hers the moment it was ready. Now she realized the foolishness of that assumption.

They were husband and wife, expected to share a bed. And even if the idea did make Rowan feel so nervous that the bread turned to stone in her belly, she immediately understood the necessity of it. The weather that day was as good a reminder as any that Scottish springtime could be unpredictable. They would need each other's warmth to settle into the night, for though the rain had abated in the last few minutes, she had no doubt it would fall stronger than ever as soon as the sun went down.

It might be nice to be curled against him, she reminded herself. And hadn't she just been longing for his touch? Surely this was the perfect opportunity to enjoy more of Lachlan's soft, chaste caresses.

She smiled as she imagined him wrapping her into his strong chest, his arms encircling her, protecting her, keeping her safe as his soft breathing lulled her into a restful, pleasant slumber.

"Lass? Do ye want any of this dried meat?" Lachlan asked, and Rowan did not bother to hide the dreamy look on her face as she shook her head.

"Nay. I think I'm ready for sleep now."

15

Lachlan awakened in the early hours of dawn, his body so attuned to its schedule that even now, it did not stray from its strict hours. But when he opened his eyes and looked at the plaid ceiling above him, at first, he was confused.

Where am I? he wondered, for the ceiling of his room at the castle was certainly not the plaid pattern he saw atop him. It was dark, grey stone, and he had looked at that ceiling nearly every day for the last fifteen years, for though he was called away to hunts and the occasional issue in the village that left him far from his bed late into the night, he had always preferred to ride back to the castle rather than sleep elsewhere. Castle Morcoille was his to protect, as were its inhabitants, and he grew uneasy if he was away for too long.

But now, as his eyes adjusted to the weak light and he looked down at his chest, he saw the dark strands of curls that topped his favorite face in this world or the next and remembered that he was on his honeymoon, asleep in a tent made of plaid with his wife quite literally by his side. Though they had fallen asleep with a hand's width between them, sometime in the night, Rowan had curled into him. Now, her head was resting on his chest, one cheek against the fabric of his shirt. Her left arm was slung across his belly as though it were the most natural thing in the world, the way she slept every night, and this warmed him to his very core.

Her waking self might not be truly comfortable in his presence, but it was clear her sleeping self was different. In sleep, she was tame as a newborn lamb and just as trusting. The sight of her resting against him roused feelings of love for her so strong they hit him like a wave, threatening to suck him into the undertow, and he watched the rise and fall of her chest, feeling like the luckiest man in the world that this was the sight that would greet him each day for the rest of his life.

Of course, this was not the first time he had

shared a bed with a lass; indeed, there were a few women in the village whom he had shared pleasures with, but nothing could compare to the bliss he was now experiencing at the sight of his Rowan snuggled tight to him. He took more pleasure from this than from all those encounters combined, for this was the culmination of a years-long infatuation that he had rarely let himself feel the full force of. It had been easier to let his love for her form a backdrop to his life, rather than command the foreground.

But now, all alone with her in his arms, Lachlan let himself fall completely into his adoration of her, going so far as to lean toward her and press a kiss to the top of her silken hair, pausing to inhale the now-familiar scent of honey and dewy green grass. It was pure ambrosia, sweet yet strong, just like her.

The silken strands of her hair tickled his face, and Lachlan smiled.

This will be our everyday. This is me new life, he reminded himself, for it seemed surreal even now. He had rejoiced so many times over the last two days that Rowan was now his, and yet it was still unbelievable that he was tied to this beautiful creature for the rest of his life. To be alone with her was a blessing in and of itself, but he hoped that as they made their way to Inverness, they would learn more about each other, would grow closer. Perhaps, in time, she might even act in her waking life as she did in sleep, allowing him to care for her, to let him see the side of her that was not surrounded by brick walls and turrets.

As he gazed at her soft sleeping form, Lachlan felt a hunger in him, not for food, but for knowledge, knowledge of Rowan. He wanted to know everything about this woman. He wanted to ken her likes and dislikes, her memories both good and bad. She was a book he had barely begun to read but whose phrasing was so enthralling that his fingers fairly shook with the need to turn the pages and find out what surprises were contained in each chapter.

For if there was one thing he knew about Rowan, it was that she would never stop surprising him.

As though she could hear his thoughts, Rowan stirred in her sleep, turning further into him, lifting her left leg and curling it around his right. Grinning even wider, Lachlan wrapped his arm around her shoulder more tightly, bringing her flush against him.

They rested like that for some time, her sleeping deeply against him while he dozed through the dawn. He was just starting to fall into a deeper sleep, his jaw slackening and his head lolling to the side when a sound near the tent brought him immediately out of his slumberous state.

The sound brought his mind back to that day at the armory when he had thought the wee stable lad was a threat to their lives. Rowan had accused him of reacting too strongly then, but what she did not understand was that after years of training, his urge to protect was as innate as breathing air. And when it came to protecting her, it was both instinct and love that fueled his reactions.

Now that they were alone in the dark woods, the chances of the noise outside being from something as innocuous as an innocent child, or animal, were slim indeed.

Therefore, Lachlan knew he had to investigate. He could not risk lying there and putting Rowan at risk. It meant leaving the warm cocoon of their tent, but that was a small sacrifice to pay for her safety.

Carefully he eased her off his chest and settled her back onto the makeshift pillow he had crafted using an extra blanket. She furrowed her brow and frowned in her sleep, and he immediately halted, waiting to see if she would wake, but when she simply rolled over and away from him, he breathed a sigh of relief.

Had she awakened, she would have insisted on

coming with him. And he could not allow that. He knew that she was capable, but hundreds of years of chivalry and a lifetime as a guard would not allow him to let his wife fight at his side. It was his duty to protect her, not the other way round.

Lachlan quickly laced on his boots and crept toward the front of his tent, and as he did so, he could feel anger beginning to stir in him and lick through his veins, heating him from head to toe. The fire grew only greater when he paused and turned back to look at the vulnerable, prone form of Rowan.

How dare someone disturb us, he thought as he reached for his sporran and extracted the dirk from within.

He would deal with whatever awaited him outside quickly, and then, he would get back to the matter of dozing with his wife, as a man should on his honeymoon. He would not let whatever or whoever was outside ruin this perfect morning.

Creeping toward the front of the tent, Lachlan lifted the edge of the fabric just enough to peek outside. The light was strong enough now to illuminate the sight of a dark-haired man standing ten feet away, next to the horses, which Lachlan had tied to a tree the night before.

The man was tall and strong, with broad shoulders and powerful calves brushing against his kilt. He was standing confidently with a straight back and looked completely at ease, as though he belonged in the woods. But no one belonged in the forest at this time of the morning.

Looking down, Lachlan noticed the man's shoes. They were fine leather brogues and looked nearly new thanks to the shining buckle atop them, which was freshly polished despite the muck and mud of the ground.

He's rich, then, Lachlan surmised.

Only someone with wealth could afford shoes like that and a person to shine them. Lachlan was about to exhale, relieved that the stranger was likely not nearly strong or skilled enough to put up much of a fight.

Before seeing the shoes, he had worried the man might be a highwayman with a crew somewhere nearby, plotting to steal what possessions of his and Rowan's they could in order to sell for a profit. Such men also had a penchant for treating women like chattel, roughly stealing the jewelry from their fingers at best, trying to abscond with them at their side at the worst. But then he realized, *if he is nae a highwayman, what is he doing in our camp?*

It was just after sunrise, in a dense bit of forest

miles from anywhere else. It was too dark to hunt, and unless the man was a healer like Blair MacManus and her mother—unlikely, as healers were usually female—the man had no business here. Which meant his main purpose must be mischievous in nature.

Tightening his grip on the dirk, Lachlan snuck out of the tent and was on the stranger before he had time to react. He drew the man's arms behind his back and brought the dirk to his throat, close enough to make the man sweat but not so much so that he would draw blood. He did not want to harm the man—not yet, at least. For now, he only wanted to scare the truth of his presence out of him.

"Who are ye, and what business do ye have in these woods?" Lachlan growled into the stranger's ear.

As he spoke, he inched them away from the horses and the tent, eager not to scare the animals or wake Rowan with what he hoped would be a swift interaction that ended with the man running in the opposite direction, back to his valet and his boot polish.

"I could ask ye the same question, for these are nay yer woods to inhabit," the man spat back, struggling against Lachlan's grip. He was strong. That was clear from the way he strained against Lachlan's hands. In response, Lachlan tightened the grasp on his wrists, forcing the stranger to bend further backward and upsetting his balance just enough that, should he succeed in ripping his hands free, he would immediately fall to the ground, making it easy for Lachlan to place a boot on his chest to stop him going any further.

In fact, he rather liked that idea, for his boots were now muddy, and marring the stranger's crisp, bright white shirt would bring him great satisfaction.

He liked the idea even more when he noticed the mocking smile curling the corners of the stranger's mouth.

He is nae taking me as a threat, Lachlan thought, instinctively pressing harder on the dirk and making the man squirm. No one underestimated him. He was Laird Campbell's head guard, the strongest hunter and best archer for miles around Castle Morcoille, and he would not let this man think him anything less than a threat to his very life.

"I'll ask ye again to answer me query, or I shall press this dirk hard enough to draw blood to drip down and stain yer fine shirt," Lachlan said, dropping his voice to allow a sinister rasp to coat his words.

The man huffed an annoyed breath, but at the infinitesimally harder press of the dirk against his throat, he answered the question. "These woods back up to me father's land."

"Aye, and who is yer father?" Lachlan asked.

"Laird MacDonald," the stranger replied. At this, Lachlan stilled.

Laird MacDonald was well known for miles around as a disgrace. After inheriting his title and land from his father, he had proceeded to destroy his family's good name by squandering the family fortune on gambling and drink, betting against his debts, and losing with such regularity that in only ten years, he was near destitute. Abducting and marrying a wealthy Englishwoman had helped matters somewhat, but soon he had spent all of her money, too. There had been uprisings from his tenant farmers and the nearby village people, who were tired of living without the protection a laird was supposed to provide for his people. His son Andrew was his last hope of recouping their money and instilling some peace among the people.

Andrew was, therefore, the man currently trying to wiggle out of Lachlan's grip. He was of an age to take a wife and had attended the annual games at Castle Morcoille, lost in the first round of the archery contest, and been found sometime in the late evening by the guards on duty, attempting to lure a kitchen maid into a dark corner near the servants' entrance to the castle.

He was, in summary, a dastardly rogue of the worst sort. The young guard Bernard had told Lachlan that as they led Andrew out to the road, he had grown agitated, screaming that he had come all the way to "this pathetic excuse for a castle" in order to win Rowan's hand and that, as she had chosen Lachlan for her husband, she lacked "even the sense of an ass," and he was well-shod of her.

"Pleased to make yer acquaintance, Andrew. Now can ye tell me why yer prowling around me camp?" Lachlan asked.

"These lands are practically me father's, and therefore practically me own since I will one day take his place. As such, I can patrol them at will to ensure that they do not become inhabited by vermin or other such unwanted creatures as yerself." Andrew was still wiggling, trying to struggle out of Lachlan's hold.

"Seeing as the land is nae yers nor yer father's,

I'll thank ye to leave the forest and let me get back to what was turning out to be quite a fine morning."

Lachlan knew the chances of a rogue like Andrew quietly slinking away were small indeed, yet he prayed to God above the man would act out of his character and depart. He did not want a fight. All he wanted was to be back in the tent with Rowan.

He felt Andrew shake his head, then heard him give a bitter laugh.

"Nay, I donnae think I can do that," Andrew said as he shoved his leg backward, clearly aiming for Lachlan's more sensitive nether area.

Lachlan deftly avoided the strike, but another came soon after, this one at his ankle. Andrew succeeded in hitting him, and though Lachlan reacted by lifting Andrew and his flailing legs off the ground, this left his ribs exposed, and Andrew jabbed his elbow into them.

Lachlan cringed, loosening his grip just enough for Andrew to free himself, though in doing so, he grazed his shoulder against the dirk, and Lachlan smiled as he saw a line of blood appear beneath the man's shirt, staining the white just as he had imagined.

Quickly righting himself, Lachlan fished another

dirk from his boot and crouched into a fighting position, prepared to strike.

Andrew had grabbed a fallen branch on his way to the forest floor, and now he stood, wielding the branch like an oversized sword.

"What is it ye truly want with me, Andrew? For I doubt verra much ye would get up so early simply to harass a single man out of the castle's neighboring woods," Lachlan said, shuffling to one side and then the other, wincing as the movement jostled his bruised ribs.

"I want ye out of these woods, and I want ye to leave me yer finery," Andrew said, lunging forward at Lachlan.

Lachlan spun on his heel and avoided the shot, though he used his fisted hand to knock at the branch, tearing off a foot of its length with his bare hands.

He heard Andrew's growl of annoyance and saw the man's already apparent temper slowly rise, a menacing glare replacing the playful glint that had colored his blue eyes thus far.

"Me finery? Are ye now so lacking in money that ye'd want even the possessions of a castle guard? Yer family must be low indeed," he told Andrew with a forced chuckle.

He knew he was baiting him, but he could not help it. He was growing bored of the fight, knowing that Andrew was not enough to truly challenge him but would do his utmost to draw things out long enough to make Lachlan frustrated and furious.

A growl sounded from Andrew, and he dropped his branch, walking quickly toward Lachlan with long strides.

"Donnae utter words against me family, Lachlan Stewart, for ye will regret it 'til yer dying day, and I will make sure that day is verra soon indeed," Andrew said, taking another step closer to Lachlan.

Lachlan realized that he had one of two choices —stay and fight Andrew or volunteer to leave. The second option was infinitely preferable, for it meant that he and Rowan could find a more hospitable stretch of land in which to camp in peace, absent the presence of malicious, scorned soon-to-be-lairds.

"If ye truly want me to leave, Andrew, I will do so. I'd rather go somewhere me peace is nae likely to be disturbed," Lachlan said.

"Yer peace?" Andrew said with a hideous laugh, the likes of which Lachlan was certain would send children crying to their mothers.

"Are ye sure it is only yer peace ye are thinking of?" he asked, closing the space between them until he was inches away from the dirk Lachlan still held in front of him in defense.

"For there are two horses just there," Andrew said, nodding at the animals placidly watching them both from their perch near the tent, "and if I am nae mistaken, two logs by yer fire pit. Are ye mayhaps traveling with a companion? Someone I might ken?" Andrew asked, but the knowing squint of his eyes told Lachlan that he already knew the answer to the question, that he was baiting him just as Lachlan had done to him.

But while it might not have been chivalrous to make jests at the expense of a man's lost family fortune, it was only the very worst man who would threaten another's wife. And that was exactly what Andrew MacDonald was doing.

Though Lachlan was indeed shocked, he kept the true depth of this feeling to himself, instead letting only a surface representation of it flash across his face, just enough to convince Andrew that he had succeeded in shaking him.

Andrew smirked, clearly pleased with himself, and Lachlan took this opportunity to lunge at him, tackling him to the ground.

As he looked down at his opponent, Lachlan wished he could rip the frustrating smirk on

Andrew's face clean off. He had been threatened countless times in his life, and never once had he felt even a shiver of fear, for he knew beyond a doubt that he could protect himself.

This was, however, the first time anyone had ever threatened Rowan in front of him, and the combination of fear and fury that flooded him now was overwhelming.

It was as his thoughts turned to Rowan that another sound came from behind Lachlan, and he turned to see five more men enter the forest, armed with dirks and swords and looking bloodthirsty.

"Ye dinnae think I would come on me own, did ye, Lachlan Stewart? As a castle guard, ye ought to ken that a laird's offspring should always travel with protection. And I dare say that ye will nae be able to offer Laird Campbell's daughter the protection she will need," Andrew said with a laugh, his chest vibrating against Lachlan's boot.

His words hit Lachlan like an arrow of ice.

I cannae protect her. Not from six men, he realized, a crushing fear accompanying this thought.

What do I do?

16

———

The deer was so near her she could almost smell the musk and earth of his coat, but she did not shoot. Not yet. She had been waiting in the tree for over three hours, and her legs had long since gone numb, but she stayed still, knowing that patience would reward her with the largest buck she had ever hunted.

The deer took two steps forward, one back, as it nosed at shrubbery on the ground.

Nearly there. One more step was all she needed. Raising her bow and slowly, silently drawing her arrow, she prepared to release, anticipating the soft thud of metal hitting bone. Her fingers were still and tensed as her elbow drew back as far as it could go before hitting the rough bark of the tree trunk behind her. But before she could let the arrow loose to fly through the air and hit its target, a commotion erupted behind her.

Male grunts and the sound of bodies crashing together suddenly overwhelmed the sylvan silence. Three men rolled into view, nearly hitting the buck with flailing limbs. The animal immediately sprinted away, but the annoyance of all those careful hours wasted was lost as Rowan leaned forward on the branch and peered down, recognizing the head of the man who was now pinned to the forest floor.

Lachlan. His hair stood out amidst the murky brown leaves, but it was not the only part of him that shined through the muck. There was also a large, angry red gash slicing across one of his eyes. Moving her gaze over the rest of his constantly moving form, Rowan saw that his elbow was bent at an unnatural angle, and he was wincing as he tried to kick the men beating him. Rowan raised her bow up again and, without a second thought, let an arrow loose from her quiver, hitting the boot of the man who had been about to lay a hard kick to Lachlan's ribs. The satisfaction of the arrow as it buried itself in the leather was short-lived, however, for another man came into view, this one with an axe, his scream of rage as he ran toward Lachlan, sending the animals that had not yet vacated the area flying, crawling, and running away.

It was Rowan's own gasp that roused her from

the dream. She opened her eyes to find the tent filled with weak light, disoriented at the swift transition from sleeping to waking. There was a fine sweat on her brow, her hair was tangled beneath her, and her heart was beating as though she had been running for miles. She was not a stranger to nightmares, had suffered from them ever since her mother died, but usually, a few minutes spent slowing down her breath banished the distress from her mind and the racing pace from her heart. However, when she tried this now, it did nothing to help her, for she could still hear the noises from her dream outside.

The grunts and yells echoed nearby, sounding only feet away.

Am I still dreaming? she wondered as she sat up and patting herself down, pinching her arm and tugging at her hair. These tricks had usually worked to wake her up, but now, nothing happened. She remained where she was, hoping that a few moments of stillness would allow her to fully awaken, but the noises persisted.

Frustrated, she shuffled to the front of the tent and drew the tent flap back. What she saw informed her that she was correct in thinking she was not asleep any longer. But what she saw was indeed the stuff of nightmares.

Ahead of her were six tall, burly men, their shoulders twice the width of her own. They were wearing a plaid unfamiliar to her, their muscular legs spread wide, some of them with arms crossed and looks of mirth on their faces.

They formed a circle, and Rowan's face drained of his normal rosy color when she saw who was in the middle—Lachlan.

She would recognize that head of hair anywhere.

Lachlan was crouched in a fighting stance and repeatedly pivoting, clearly trying to avoid blind spots that would leave him vulnerable to attack. But as Rowan looked closer through a gap between two of the larger men, it became clear that even if Lachlan had eyes in the back of his head, they would not aid him. For as he turned in her direction, she saw that he was wounded, though not in the way she had dreamed. Instead, it was far worse.

One of his eyes was so black and swollen she could not even see the lid, and the other bore a large, deep cut just below it that traveled the length of his bearded cheek, from the bottom of his nose to just above his temple. He was leaning heavily to one side, and Rowan surmised that one of his ankles must be sprained at the least or possibly broken at the very worst.

He was in no state to fight the men crowding him alone, and yet as she hastily gathered her bag and tied her shoes, she watched Lachlan continue to deflect punches, kicks, and swipes with a sword she was almost certain he had stolen from one of his attackers, for she had not seen it among their belongings. His skills allowed him to avoid the worst of the violence, but she could see he was growing tired, his strength waning.

I have to help him, else he might be killed, she thought, and the very idea of someone harming him further sent her sprinting out of the tent with one last weapon in hand.

As she ran, she did not pause to think about the repercussions of her actions. She did not consider whether it might not be the best idea to go up against six men on her own. Lachlan was hurt, and she needed to protect him. It was instinct.

As she neared the circle, she momentarily slowed, readying her bow and the first of a fistful of arrows which she'd plunged into the soft soil near her feet. When she looked up, her eyes met with Lachlan's.

His eyes widened with shock at the sight of her, then grew bigger, his pupils darting off to the side.

Rowan knew that he was telling her to stay away,

but she ignored his directive. Staying away would not protect him, and that is what she had come to do.

Memories of the many mornings she'd spent in practice came back to her in a rush. Little had she known at the time what she'd been practicing for.

The first arrow hit its mark with ease. Yet she'd never heard a surprised scream coming from one of the targets on the practice ground. The man fell to his knees, struggling wildly at the arrow now embedded in his shoulder, unable to reach it.

This created chaos, with Lachlan's attackers ceasing their efforts in favor of looking about to see what had taken place. They hadn't counted on being felled by a capable lass. She reached down, pulling another arrow from the ground and nocking it quickly, taking aim at a second man. A third. They fell screaming, swearing, clutching their injured shoulders and arms.

There was no thought involved. No strategy. Fell them, protect Lachlan. It was all that mattered, the only goal in mind. By the time her thinking cleared and the threat was lessened, there were six men strewn about, all of them in pain.

She'd wounded them. This was her doing. Yet

there could be no guilt involved, for it had been they who'd chosen to attack her husband.

Her husband who seemed as surprised as the rest. "Lass? What are ye doing?" he asked once she reached him.

Before, she had only caught glimpses of his face, but having the chance to view it up close made her protective instincts swell all over again, accompanied by something else—anger. Lachlan looked exactly as expected for someone who had tried to fight off six men by himself. In addition to his facial wounds, he was also hugging his side, indicating bruised or broken ribs.

How dare those men wound him, she thought as she looked back at the supposed warriors now writhing in pain. Three of them appeared to have lost consciousness, likely from loss of blood after they'd been foolish enough to carelessly tear the arrows from their flesh and thus worsen their wounds, while the other half attempted to crawl away before she could strike again. She felt the urge to kick each and every one of them but refrained because, unlike them, she did not believe it was a fair fight if one's opponent could not properly defend themselves.

"What did ye do, lass?" Lachlan asked, and

Rowan turned back to him, laying a hand on his cheek as she stepped closer. She touched him so she could turn his face to the side and properly inspect his wound, but she also needed to feel him, to feel the warmth of his skin and the reminder of blood continuing to pump through his veins. She needed the reminder that while he might be injured, he was still alive.

"How—?" she asked as she looked at the cut on his cheek. It was deeper than she had first thought and would need cleaning and stitching. But rather than answer her, Lachlan jerked away from her.

"Answer me questions first, lass. What did ye think ye were doing?"

Rowan huffed, frustrated that he was still focusing on the fight when what they ought to be focusing on was healing him.

"Ye can still see, aye? What does it appear I did? I ended the fight." She took his arm and lead him to a tree near the tent with the moans and grunts of the wounded men still ringing in her ears.

He was too bemused to argue at being led like a child, nor did he refuse her help as she settled him at the base of a tree whose roots were conveniently curved so that he could elevate his injured ankle as he sat.

"Ye cannae leave them this way." Lachlan looked back over the sight of the battle. "They will not take kindly to knowing a lass felled them once they regain their strength."

She saw the truth of this soon enough. Already the strongest of the men was struggling to get to his feet in spite of an arrow embedded in his thigh and another in his left shoulder. He must have struck his head on falling, for a cut there dripped blood into his eyes.

Yet still he endeavored to right himself. The others were on the ground and appeared prepared to give up the fight—it took nothing for a coward to fight when he knew his opponent was outnumbered, but this was another matter altogether.

"Wait here." She dug through her bag while darting over to the men, stepping over those who'd lost consciousness before reaching the struggling attacker. She used his head wound to her advantage, knowing he could scarcely see anything thanks to the blood in his eyes, yet she was intensely aware of the danger of being this near to him. She would only have one chance to get this right.

Luck was on her side. She unstopped the sleeping draught whose qualities Mary MacManus had taught her. One drop would be enough to send a grown man into nearly immediate sleep. She could hardly afford to take chances, though, especially with a large and evidently strong opponent who might now be intent on killing them both if only for revenge.

He might have killed Lachlan. The thought bolstered her, giving her the courage to take a handful of the man's hair and pull his head back. He reacted at once, his mouth falling open as he prepared to scream any number of foul things. She took the opportunity to tip the small bottle over his mouth, allowing several drops of the draught to hit his tongue before releasing him and backing away.

The mixture had its intended effect and in a matter of moments, the man fell to the side and went still. So still, in fact, that Rowan feared she'd stopped his heart. When his chest rose she allowed herself a sigh of relief before rejoining her husband.

"I'll clean and stitch up the cut on yer cheek first, and then I'll tend to the rest of ye," she said, ignoring his question as she took a bottle out of her bag. Leaning toward him, she gently dabbed the concoction around the gash.

Lachlan stared at her as she worked, waiting for the salve to numb the area before taking out a needle and thread and beginning to sew the skin closed.

When she was done, she put the thread and needle back in the bag and took out various ointments and balms to help with Lachlan's other bruises and sprains.

"What else do ye have in that bag? It seems bottomless," Lachlan croaked, his voice hoarse as he peered at her with his good eye.

"Healing supplies," she answered as she began to smooth ointment over his bruised eye. It was already turning from red to purple, the lid swollen shut and twice its normal size. It would be at least a day before he could open the eye again, maybe more.

"We cannae leave them this way." He insisted upon turning his head away from her as she worked. "We must rid ourselves of them now. My wounds can wait."

He was stubborn, but Rowan could see the truth of this. She no longer had surprise on her side. "What do ye suggest?" It was the right thing to say, for she suspected he hardly appreciated being rescued by a woman—wife or nae—and needed to feel she relied on his wisdom now.

"We could tie them to their horses. I assume they rode here, though I neither saw nor heard a sign of the animals. I suppose that was by design." Yes, they would wish to surprise him as she'd surprised them. The cowardly things.

"I expect they'd be tied off some distance away, perhaps at the edge of the forest, where we entered last night." He nodded his head to the west.

"Then we tie them to their horses and send the horses off to carry them back from whence they came," Rowan said.

"A perfect plan, lass, though I am afraid I will nae be much help what with all the..." He gestured at himself, his bloodied clothes, bruised face and throat, his injured ankle.

"If ye can hold the men steady on their horses, I shall do the tying and leading them away," Rowan said, smiling at him, pleased to be once again handling the more difficult aspects of the situation.

"I cannae think of a better person for the job," he told her with pride in his voice.

It took some time for Rowan to find the horses and lead them back, for, as was the case with most animals, they were loyal to their owners and distrusting of strangers. She had taken a few apples and carrots out of their own animals' feed bags, and by the time she returned, the fruit and vegetables were gone, already being slowly digested by the stroppy animals she was leading behind her.

While she was gone, Lachlan had untangled some of the rope they had brought with them and carefully tied the wrists of each man, leaving a tail of rope that Rowan could tie to around the men's ankles and attach to their saddles, so they did not fall off their horses. "Did they try to fight ye?" she asked upon reaching them, the horses behind her.

"Nay, ye managed to rid them of the desire to fight." In fact, only one of the men was still awake and aware, and he was far too concerned with the arrow embedded deep in his hind area to pay heed to his captors. Indeed, blood covered his entire leg and still dripped onto the ground, though it would not if only he would remain still. "I suspect the fact it was a lass who felled him hurts a great deal worse."

Lachlan could pull the men to their feet but could not life them onto their saddles, and so he watched as Rowan did so, bracing each man across her shoulders and hefting him onto the saddle before righting him. "How do ye manage it?" he asked with awe in his voice.

"It needs to be done." That was all she could say before arranging the next man and tying him securely in place. It needed to be done, just as defending her husband needed to be done. There was no limit to what she was capable of when it came to him.

It seemed he breathed far easier even with injured ribs once they had sent the men on their way, their horses making a slow trot up the hill. Rowan's relief, though real, was short-lived. "Now, 'tis yer turn."

Lachlan laughed, the chuckle turning into a cough that had him wincing and clutching his side. Rowan sat him back down and looked at him with concern.

"I think I shall go the rest of me life, and never a day shall pass when ye do nae amaze me, lass."

She smiled at this compliment, though her smile quickly faded when she noticed the rough quality of his normally smooth, deep voice. Gently bending toward him, she inspected his neck, feeling along to where she could find some tenderness.

"Were ye hit in the throat?" she asked as she moved her hands down to his rib, lifting up his shirt to inspect his ribs.

"Aye. By Andrew MacDonald," he said as Rowan inspected the large contusion spread across four of his lower ribs. "It was his mouth ye poured that sleeping draught into."

At that name, her hands paused in their inspection, and she lifted her head, her brow furrowing. "That name sounds familiar," she said, shutting her eyes as she tried to remember where she had heard it. When she could not find the answer, she opened her eyes and looked at Lachlan as she asked, "Who is he? And why did he attack ye?"

It struck her as she waited for his answer that in the time she had spent first fighting for Lachlan and then healing him, she had not once considered the reason for the sudden attack on him. She had simply reacted to it, knowing she needed to stop it, to help him, to keep him away from any more harm. But now, she sat back on her heels, waiting for Lachlan to tell her the story before she continued to heal him.

"He wanted to marry ye," Lachlan said, clearing his throat. "He was at the annual games hoping to woo ye and was angry when it was I ye had chosen as yer betrothed. His father owns the land next to the forest, and he must have found out we were headed this way from a mutual acquaintance of his father and yers. He wanted to beat me senseless until I could nae protect ye and then steal ye away."

"Steal me away? When I'm already yer wife?

What sense does that make?" she said with a disbe-lieving laugh.

"An annulment, lass," Lachlan explained. "His family may be in disgrace, but they still hold enough power in these parts to convince a priest to do such a thing. The MacDonalds are verra good at using people for their own ends."

Shocked, Rowan still managed to ask, "How did ye ken all this?"

"He told me. Right after his men crowded around me, said he saw no reason a man should perish not knowing the reason for his death," Lachlan said.

17

The thought of Lachlan nearly dying almost had Rowan on her knees. She had only really started to let him in, to let him truly ken her, and the idea of losing him was enough to send tears to her eyes.

"I cannae believe it," she said, wiping at them before they could spill. "I cannae believe he threatened ye like that. Just for me hand."

"It was nae merely for yer hand, lass. If ye remember, his family is in desperate need of money, which ye readily have from yer father. Betrothing ye would have been a means to an end for him," Lachlan said, and she saw that he was struggling with his own set of strong emotions at the thought of their separation.

Rowan wanted to ask more questions, to wonder how Andrew had expected her father to so readily hand over money to a man he knew was not one she had chosen for her husband, but she paused when she saw the true depth of sadness in her mate's eyes. He looked distraught, as though the very idea of her being taken away from him had ripped apart his soul.

She could feel tears threatening anew, and she drew her hand up to once again wipe beneath her eyes. But just before her fingertips met the delicate skin below her lashes, she realized Andrew's threat to Lachlan's life could have been avoided with one simple action.

"If ye kenned it was his plan to kill ye, why did ye nae call to me?" she asked. "Why did ye nae shout to me for help?"

Lachlan balked as though she had struck him. "Called to ye? Why would I call ye out to face a murderous, dangerous man and his six henchmen?"

"Because they were going to kill ye. And I could have protected ye. If I had entered the fray even a few minutes before I did, ye might be saved some of those bumps and bruises," she said, nodding at the various injuries scattered across the map of his body.

Lachlan shook his head. "Nay, lass. I dinnae need

yer help. I was doing a fine job of defending the both of us before ye arrived, and I would have beaten them if ye had nae come out when ye did," he told her defensively.

"Aye?" Rowan said, raising her eyebrows in mock surprise. "So ye think ye would have been fine fighting off six men while ye were limping and leaning to one side, strength going out of yer bones with every breath ye took?" Not waiting for him to respond, she continued. "How is it that ye thought letting yerself be beaten until ye were helpless, or worse, dead, could be defined as defending us both?"

Rowan knew the words would sting, but she did not care, for in characterizing her aid as unnecessary, Lachlan had not only hurt her but had confirmed her worst fears, which just last night she had begun to let fade from her mind, mollified by their conversation before the wedding and his actions toward her in the days after.

He does nae really think me his equal. He does nae believe in me strength.

She felt sick to her stomach at the thought that she had so gravely misjudged the man before her.

"Helpless?" Lachlan replied, his voice only a

hair's breadth away from shouting. "Do ye mean to call me weak, lass?"

He tried to stand, but even the effort of sitting up had him wincing in pain. At the sight of his struggle, Rowan had to pretend ignorance to the screams within her body begging her to reach out to him, to take him in her arms, and press kisses to his unharmed cheek as she slowly pushed him back into a reclining position better for his injuries. Instead, she held firm, burying those feelings deeper than Castle Morcoille's loch.

"Nae, I'm calling ye a bampot whose pride blinded him to the truth of the situation," she retorted, crossing her arms.

"And by truth, ye mean that I would have lost that fight had ye nae intervened?" he asked, grabbing her hand and bringing her toward him.

Rowan stumbled and nearly fell into his lap, only saving herself from that fate by bracing herself with a hand to his chest and her knees straddling his, bringing their chests practically crushed together.

Mere hours ago, this touch would have lit a fire of want and pleasure within her, would have had her mind racing off with the relentless need for more of his touch, but now, it only reminded her just how foolish she had been to let herself fall for him. How stupidly she had preened at his attention the night before, thinking herself lucky that she had such a husband.

I should nae have let down me guard around him. I should nae have trusted him to be anything other than a thoughtless man.

"Aye, ye would have lost, and a better man would admit it rather than trying to convince himself otherwise. A better man would confess when he needed help, rather than needlessly risk his own life and mine to save his pride," she snarled back.

"Then I am sorry to disappoint ye, lass, for I ken ye thought ye chose the best man for the job of husband, but I will admit nae such thing," he whispered back. There was anger in his tone, but sadness, too, echoed in his eyes as he tried to catch her gaze. "I am nae the better man yer asking for."

Rowan refused to look at him, however, knowing that one glance into the emerald depths of his irises would weaken her beyond repair. She would apologize and even, perhaps, reach out and take his lips, quieting him with a press of their mouths. But it would not solve the problem they were now faced with, which was that her husband clearly did not understand her or her needs.

Pushing off his chest, she backed away from him, standing up and putting as much distance as she could between herself and the tree he was seated beneath. With every footstep, she found her strength, her resolve returning.

When she looked back at Lachlan, he was leaning against the tree, his eyes shut, his face scrunched, whether in concentration or consternation, she could not tell.

She let the silence linger between them, needing time to gather her thoughts.

And as she did so, she realized that the foolishness had not been in trusting Lachlan, but in expecting that on day two of their marriage and when faced with a crisis, he would immediately abandon all the teachings his family and society had taught him about the ways of being a husband.

He needed time to get to know her and to grow into being the partner she needed, just as she too required time to learn to talk rather than argue when faced with a difficult situation.

Arguing was, after all, a form of ignorance, and as Lachlan had so sagely said the morning of their wedding, they needed to meet their problems rather than ignoring them.

They could not go on hurting each other, not

when they were now all each other had. They could not spend the rest of their honeymoon in anger, nor did she want to. If she wanted Lachlan to see her side of things, to make him understand how and why he had hurt her, she could only do so with a calm temperament and kind words.

Clearing her throat, she closed some of the space she had put between them, not missing Lachlan's eyes following every movement toward him that her body took.

"The morning of our wedding, ye promised me ye would let me do as I please. That ye would nae try to change me. When ye said that... I started to believe that I might one day be able to love ye the way ye love me because ye loved me as I am. But just now, when ye would nae admit that I helped ye, that I protect ye, I thought it was because ye would nae have a wife who did those things. And that is the only kind of wife I can be," she said, looking down at her hands and fidgeting, for she could not bear the heat of his stare on her just then.

"I cannae help but want to protect ye, Lachlan. Yer me husband. And I want ye to see that part of me and love it as much as ye profess to love the rest of me," she said, dropping her point of focus to the ground.

"I love ye, Rowan Campbell, exactly as ye are. I meant it then, and I mean it now. I love each and every part of ye," he said, and Rowan looked up to find him pleading her closer with his gaze. She took a step toward him, then another, until her boots were touching his.

"But when it comes to protecting ye, to keep ye safe…" he shook his head, wiping his hand over his jaw. "There is naught I would nae do to look after ye. I thought I could handle Andrew and his men on me own. I thought if I could nae, then I should nae be yer father's head guard nor yer husband, for surely a better man could have handled both."

"Ye are the best man I could have hoped for, Lachlan Stewart," Rowan said, and this time, she allowed herself to kiss him, to crawl to his side and take his face in her hands, meeting his shocked smile with a wicked one of her own.

The kiss, though chaste, communicated more feeling than either of them could have ever put into words, and it left Rowan breathless. When her lips left his, she leaned her forehead against his, needing a moment to come back to a land where she did not only dwell in dreams.

When she sat back, she was treated to the sight of Lachlan smiling at her, his eyes alight with a happiness that brightened their dark green to the hue of leaves after a cleansing spring rain.

Taking his hand in hers and intertwining their fingers together, she said, "I ken ye want to keep me safe. But ye must understand, Lachlan, that just as ye feel that instinct for me, so I feel it for ye. I think all women feel it for their husbands, but many are nae able to act on it. But I am."

"Aye. When I heard what Andrew was planning, I dinnae want to call to ye and risk endangering yerself," Lachlan said.

At that, Rowan rolled her eyes. "When I heard the sound of fighting outside the tent and saw ye surrounded by those men, I dinnae stop to think whether I might be endangering meself. All I kenned was that protecting ye was the most important thing in the world at that moment. My body moved before me mind even kenned what I was doing or where I was going."

"As did mine when I heard Andrew outside our tent," he admitted. "I was so angry at him for disturbing the peace I'd found with ye curled around me in the tent that I dinnae think anything of sneaking up on him and trying to scare him into fleeing."

Rowan's breath caught at the mention of the two

of them snuggled together. Though she did not consciously remember entwining her body with his, it made sense, for just before the nightmare began, she had been in the same setting, sitting in the same tree watching the same buck, only she was not alone. Lachlan had been behind her, his arms circled around her waist, his chin resting on her shoulder as he whispered humorous tales of the time before he lived at the Castle, back when he was part of the Stewart clan.

"If our time together was as blissful as the dreams it inspired, then I can well understand what made ye rush Andrew without a second thought," she told him, nuzzling her nose against his.

"It was the best morning of me life. Up until Andrew arrived," he said with a laugh.

"It might take time for ye to see that I am as capable of caring for ye as ye are for me, but ye must. I cannae stand to be thought of as useless in a crisis. The next time a man attacks us, God forbid, I want to be by yer side from the first," she said, squeezing his hand and adding, "Nae matter how uncomfortable that idea might make ye."

Lachlan pursed his lips but dipped his chin, communicating his acquiescence.

"I can do that. It might take time before it comes

naturally, but I promise I will do so, lass. I... I suppose I can admit that without yer help, I would nae have fared near so well with those men," he said, reaching up and feeling the newly stitched gash on his cheek. "Without ye, I might have died."

"Let that yer aches and pains be a lesson to ye then," Rowan said.

"Though I ought to finish caring for yer ribs and ankle before the pain gets any worse," she said and reluctantly got off his lap to retrieve her bag of healing potions.

She worked in silence as she bandaged up his ribs and ankle, but this time it was not an uncomfortable quiet but an easy one.

18

As Rowan tied the knot on the bandage around his ankle, Lachlan marveled at all that she could do. Incapacitate six men with nothing but a bow and arrows, set them on their saddles and send them on their way, kiss him senseless, and tend to his many wounds, all in the space of what could not have been more than an hour.

"Yer awe-inspiring, lass," he told her as she packed up her bag and tested the tightness of his bandages.

Rowan smiled and shook her head. "I'm nae angel, Lachlan."

"Nae, yer better, for in all the many times I've

been injured or hurt, nae angel has ever deigned to spend precious time healing a bampot like me."

"Clearly they dinnae ken what a handsome bampot ye are then," she teased back at him.

"Truly lass, I am grateful for all yer efforts this morning. Fighting for me, healing me. Every day I find more things to love about ye, more things that shock and delight me about ye."

He did not miss the drop in Rowan's shoulders or the brief, strong emotion that crossed her face at his words.

He knew she was still not used to his love, but he would continue to profess it forevermore, for there was no lass more deserving of it than the one before him.

It would take time for him to learn exactly what she needed of him and he of her, but he was confident with each passing day of their marriage, they would understand each other more. And if that understanding came with more of her kisses, then so much the better.

The true existence of their union struck him. It seemed that their wedding had happened weeks, even months ago, that the events of that morning were far in the past.

He was reminded of their recent nature with a

glance past Rowan's tangled hair up the hill toward the castle from which Andrew and his men had come.

"We ought to move camp early tomorrow morning, in case they send more of their men." He looked to her to see whether she agreed.

"I donnae think they will, for in doing so, they would have to reveal how they came to be tied in the first place, which would surely wound their pride, but I would rather err on the side of caution," Rowan mused.

"Aye. I would suggest we leave tonight, but I donnae think I can manage it," he said, feeling as though he had not slept or eaten in days rather than hours. "When will I start to heal?" he asked, guessing that it would not be for some time. Even holding each man steady with just one hand had taxed him far more than it ought to, and at that moment, all he craved was rest.

"The swelling in yer eye will lessen in a day or two, but I fear that yer rib and ankle will take longer, especially if ye insist on riding," she said, adding, "The angle of the stirrup will aggravate the soreness."

"What if ye ride in front and I behind ye? We can trail one of the horses. It will be slower, but we donnae have to be in Inverness with any immediacy," he said. "We can send yer father a letter when we arrive there, saying we have decided to take a few more weeks to ourselves."

"I would like that verra much, husband," Rowan said, kissing his cheek.

The combination of affectionate moniker and the feel of her lips on his skin twice in as many hours made Lachlan momentarily forget the body aches and pains, so enraptured was he with his mighty wife.

19

———

Five days later

Rowan ought to have awakened with a smile on her face and warmth in her heart. After all, the last few days with Lachlan had been truly wonderful. Though the attack and its resulting argument had been difficult, healing Lachlan and resolving the conflict between them had served to break down some of the barriers she had been holding against him. It was far easier to confide in him now that he understood her better, and Rowan had begun to relish the long, meandering conversations they had in the dark of the night when both would spill their secrets and share their innermost feelings. She had felt this closeness with only one other person in her whole life, and even Blair did not know some of the whisperings she shared with Lachlan. She trusted him completely.

She had told him of how much she missed her mother, how she wondered whether her mother would have accepted her unfeminine ways rather than shunning her as her sisters had done. She had let herself cry in front of him for the loneliness she had felt most of her life, even with Blair by her side, and Lachlan had comforted her, holding her tight in his arms as he reminded her that from now on, she would never have to feel lonely again.

"I'm here, lass. I'm here, and I always will be," he had promised, his voice deep in her ear. "Trust me."

Rowan did trust him, but now, as she was roused from yet another horrible nightmare, she realized that while her faith in her husband was unwavering, her trust in the future had vanished.

And without it, Rowan was struggling to sleep without being assaulted by violent nightmares, full of visions of Lachlan dying in gruesome ways, the life force fading out of his dark green eyes as she watched.

This morning was the fifth in as many days when she awakened crying out, tears staining her cheeks as she reached blindly for Lachlan, needing to feel his vibrant warmth against her, to remind herself that he was alive and well.

Often, he could comfort her back to sleep, but today, his touch did nothing to assuage her fears.

He cannae promise to always be here with me. Not when men like Andrew MacDonald walk the earth's grounds, she realized, her thumbs running over Lachlan's knuckles, tracing the freckles she knew the exact pattern of despite the relative darkness of the tent. She had memorized their pattern these last few days and tried to visualize them in her mind, focusing on the smattering of dots on the back of his hand, which she thought looked exactly like the constellation Orion.

It was a fitting mark for a warrior and guard. But while she knew her own strength and that of Lachlan's, she could not help but imagine a thousand scenarios in which their valor was overpowered, and Lachlan was taken from her by Andrew or his likeness in another man. His attack had reminded her that evil lurked amongst them, and she knew now, more strongly than ever, that she would not rest until they were back within the protected walls of Castle Morcoille, where she knew every cranny and corner, and nothing was unexpected.

"So, how long 'til we are back at Castle

Morcoille?" Lachlan whispered, shaking her out of her contemplations.

"What do ye mean?" she asked, playing witless for a moment, though she knew instantly by his tone and the steady shine of his gaze on her that he saw right through her mendacity.

"I mean that ye have been slowly leading us home these last few days. I might have been hit in the head, lass, but I still ken these lands, and I notice when we pass the same hills we traversed the day after our wedding. I might have been riddled with excitement then, but I am a good enough hunter to always take note of me surroundings."

Rowan huffed out a laugh and lay back down, pressing his hand between hers as she settled on her side to face him.

She had thought she was secretive, slowly guiding them back home these last three days, navigating the horses with Lachlan on the saddle behind her. The soft rocking of the horse's gait sent him to sleep for hours at a time, offering her ample time to guide them back down south and east without his being any the wiser.

"We have but one day left of riding. I went slowly, as I dinnae want to jostle yer shoulder or ankle," she said, looking at him sheepishly.

"I am nae angry, lass. I donnae need a honeymoon in Inverness with ye. To be truthful, I want to start me life with ye as soon as possible. And I shall only feel comfortable doing so once we've reported Andrew's attack to yer father and ensured the lad gets the proper punishment."

"Lad? Is he nae a man of at least thirty years of age?" Rowan asked with a laugh.

"Any male who seeks revenge on another and threatens a woman in the while does nae deserve the rank of manhood."

Rowan giggled, resting her head beneath Lachlan's chin, a spot that curved so perfectly to her form that she often wondered if God had not made them to fit together like lock and key.

"I want to start me life with ye too, Lachlan. And I agree that we cannae do so in good faith until Andrew is punished. I cannae sleep for dreams of him hurting ye again. Of... killing ye," she said, feeling elated even as emotion thickened her voice.

"I ken, and it breaks me heart to see ye wake with me name on yer lips, not in bliss but in fear. I want peace for ye. For both of us," he said, pressing his lips to the top of her hair.

"I could nae bear it if yer attacked again, Lachlan. Seeing ye hurt again will tear me heart in two. If something happens to ye again, if ye die... I will die. I cannae go on without ye, I cannae survive without yet by me side," she said, her earlier mirth replaced by an overwhelming sadness. Tears began to stream down her face, and she let them fall, unabashed.

"Och," Lachlan said, catching the tears with his lips, melting away the evidence of her sadness with each and every press of his lips against her skin.

"I love ye, Lachlan. I think I have loved ye for some time, but it is only now that I see it clearly. Ye have me heart, now and always," she whispered.

Lachlan pulled her into him, guiding her head to his chest, and Rowan turned into his soft cambric shirt, breathing in the scent of him, of wood smoke and musk, wanting nothing more than to be surrounded by him, cocooned in his warmth and love for the rest of her days.

"Ye love me," Lachlan said on a laugh, sounding incredulous.

"Aye, I do. More than I ever thought I could love anyone or anything," she confessed, resting her forehead against his heart.

"More than me bow and arrow, more than meself. I love ye more than anything else in this world," she told him, saying each word slowly, like a prayer, a benediction.

Lachlan responded by lifting her chin until her eyes met his, so she could watch as he leaned in and captured her lips.

Rowan was shocked at his touch but quickly melted into him, finding that kissing him came as naturally to her as shooting an arrow or spotting a poisonous mushroom.

"I love ye," she whispered again, breaking the kiss to rub her nose against his, adoring the taste of the words on her mouth. They were sweeter than sugar and biscuits, more fulfilling than a glass of ale and stew. They were everything she had ever needed, and in saying them, she felt peace within herself unlike any she had ever known.

20

———

Lachlan was tired from the journey despite sleeping much of the afternoon away, content to loll his head against Rowan's shoulder as she led them home. But this was not the rest of the sick or convalescing. Nay, it seemed that Rowan's confession of love was the ultimate unction, the key to healing him of his wounds. He felt stronger with each hour that passed and could almost sense his body knitting itself whole again. Rowan's love had cured him, not only of his wounds but of his arrogance, his assumptions. Never before had he let someone else take the reins, but he knew without a doubt that he had married his equal.

Nae, me better, he thought, laughing inside, for it was true that Rowan was a force, containing a multitude of strength and emotion that he would spend the rest of his life learning from and admiring.

"I want to stop at Blair's first. I want her mother to check yer wounds, to ensure I healed ye properly," Rowan told him, the first words she had spoken in some hours.

"I am sure ye've done a better job than even she, but if that is where ye would go first, lass, I shall happily be by yer side," Lachlan whispered in her ear, admiring the small, perfect pearlescent lobe before turning his eyes to the sights beyond them.

The familiar curves of the castle were just up ahead as they rounded the base of hills, headed toward the southeast corner of a glen at the edge of the castle's land.

Lachlan heard Blair's voice before he saw her running toward them, her apron flapping in the wind and her blond hair flying out of its bun.

"What in God's name are ye two doing here? Ought ye nae to be on a honeymoon in Inverness?" she asked, only just stopping when she reached the horses.

She was breathing heavily as she took Rowan's hand in hers.

"We have made a slight change of plans," Rowan said, and Lachlan could see that though she spoke nothing else, a thousand words passed between the two women in that silent way bosom friends have of communicating.

"Tea. And cake. And biscuits. Ma has just finished baking up a storm, and I'm sure she'd be delighted to share the spoils," she said, catching Lachlan's eye and smiling almost as though she could see his hunger.

Rowan had not wanted to stop for a meal today, and Lachlan had happily accepted this change in plans; he could stand an empty belly for a day if it meant they were home safe in their beds that night.

But now, after sliding off the saddle and handing the horse off to the MacManus's gardener, Raibert, to return to the castle stables, Lachlan's middle emitted a loud, pronounced growl that sent both Rowan and Blair into peals of laughter.

"It is a good thing Ma made enough to feed a crowd. I dare say ye'll eat the lot of it," Blair jested as she led them down the cottage's front path.

The smell of buttery shortbread and oatcakes fresh from the griddle assaulted Lachlan the moment he stepped into the cottage's back garden, the ambrosial odors wafting out of the cottage's open kitchen window.

"Ma. Get two extra cups out. We have visitors

for tea." Blair called as they made their way carefully down the path leading to the structure's back door.

The MacManuss had an extensive vegetable and herb garden that stretched for a quarter acre, and just behind the cottage's back wall was a small flower garden bracketing either side of a stone walkway. Already in early March, the garden was a riot of color, but Lachlan barely glanced at it, instead intent on getting to the food and the tea.

And sure enough, when they entered the kitchen, there was Mary MacManus, adding cream and a heaping teaspoon of sugar to one of the four cups on the large wooden table before her.

"This is for ye. Drink it all, or else ye will have nae biscuits," she told Lachlan in lieu of a greeting, pressing the teacup in his hand and maternally shoving him into a chair before turning to Blair and Rowan.

Lachlan noticed they were given their cups with less force, but then, perhaps Mary had heard the growl of his stomach all the way in the garden.

Lachlan relished the sweet, creamy taste of the strong brew in his hand, his first cup of tea in nearly a week. He could live without tea and had done so on countless hunts and trips back to his family's lands, but the first steaming cup of the tannic mixture was one of life's truest pleasures.

And as he looked across the table at Rowan, who was in similar rapture with her own cup, he felt completely, wholly calm.

There had been moments since the attack when he had felt so—sleeping at Rowan's back, curled around her in the dead of night, but those had been fleeting. Now, however, he allowed the feeling to settle in him, softening his frayed nerves and soothing his lingering fears.

Naught can happen to us on Castle Morcoille lands, he reminded himself as he settled back in his chair.

Mary MacManus plopped into the seat next to him, a small grunt escaping her mouth as she settled against the hard wood.

"Those are quite the bruises ye've got on yer face, Lachlan, and I daresay I detect a broken rib and sprained ankle as well. What happened to ye on yer journey, to hurt ye and leave yer wife looking so pale and tired? I would wager she had nae slept in a month if I had not seen her only a week ago," Mary said as she drew a plate of biscuits toward her and passed it to him. Her watery blue eyes were sharp and assessing as she stared at him, waiting for him to answer her questions.

Lachlan took three of the shortbread, but though he was nearly salivating for their buttery sweetness, he answered her before taking his first bite.

"We were attacked. By Andrew MacDonald, a rapscallion and rogue intent on killing me and taking Rowan for his own. He wanted her fortune. Thankfully, Rowan fought him off. It was a sight to behold, in truth. I have nae in me life seen men felled so quickly," he said with a laugh that bore no trace of humor in it. Instead, it was a laugh of disbelief.

Speaking the tale aloud was a strange experience. For nearly a week, he and Rowan had lived with the knowledge of it but had spoken of it little before yesterday. Telling of it now reminded him of the true gravity of the situation, and he felt a coldness sweep through him at the realization of how close they had been to irrevocable destruction—of their marriage, of his body—they had been.

Lachlan looked across the table at Rowan, who caught his eye and gave him a small, shy smile before turning back to Blair, who was talking animatedly, her hands waving around with such force that her tea nearly sloshed over the side of its cup.

"Marriage has many obstacles, though normally

they do nae appear quite so soon after the wedding. I am verra sorry to hear yer honeymoon was cut short, but I am glad to ken ye both are well and that Rowan has cared for ye so nicely. She is a good lass. The best, excepting me Blair," Mary told him as she sipped her tea.

"It was a wise idea to return home. The laird will take care of Andrew MacDonald and ensure yer continued safety," she added.

"Thank ye. Rowan is by far the best woman I ken, and while I trust her with me life, it does feel good to be on familiar ground again," he said, eating the last of his shortbread.

Mary reached for the oatcakes and began to butter one as she spoke.

"Yer injuries seem to be well healed from how ye sit and move. The bruise on yer eye looks far worse than it is, and I daresay that scar on yer face will only make ye more handsome in the eyes of yer wife," she said, handing him the buttered oatcake.

Lachlan laughed, gratefully accepting the cake, and biting into it.

Warm, toasted oat flavor with a hint of something he could not place assaulted his tongue.

"Oil of almond," Mary supplied, as though she

could see him trying to decipher the flavor. "I make it meself. And have taught Rowan to do the same."

Lachlan looked across the table again, this time pausing at the visage of Rowan and Blair together. They were so different in temperament, and yet it was clear there was an unbreakable bond between them. Blair brought out Rowan's less serious side, enticing her into laughter more boisterous than Lachlan had ever heard from her.

This morning, she had looked tired and in need of rest. But now, among the MacManuss, whose home he could see felt nearly as familiar to her as her own, she was relaxed, the rosy hue coming back to her cheeks and energy returning to her in the set of her shoulders as she giggled at something Blair said.

Lachlan had always had friends, but he had never before had a bosom friend, someone he could trust wholeheartedly with his secrets, good and bad. But now, he had Rowan.

She was not only his wife, but over the last week, she had become his friend as well. He confided in her and trusted her with his everything—thoughts, emotions, fears, and hopes.

"They are close as two peas in a pod," Mary MacManus muttered to him, and Lachlan turned to her with a questioning glance, wondering how she could have gleaned the nature of his expression.

"I saw ye glancing at them and wondering at their bond. It is one forged in childhood and strong enough to last a lifetime, I dare say, though now, Rowan will not need Blair so much. Not when she has ye," Mary said.

Lachlan smiled, but it was tinged with sadness for Blair. "Will she be lonely, do ye think? I've promised Rowan she can continue to heal and shoot and spend as much time as she needs in the woods, but marriage will naturally limit the time she is idle."

"Idle? That lass has nae been idle a day in her life," Mary said with a cackle.

Lachlan ducked his head in agreement, amending his statement. "It will limit her time here, with ye and Blair, healing."

Mary's grin did not waver as she said, "Blair will be just fine, Lachlan. With any hope, she too will soon experience transformation and change."

"Are ye marrying her off to someone?" Lachlan asked, careful to keep his voice low lest Blair and Rowan hear. There was little chance of this since both were still whispering excitedly, their heads bowed together.

"Nae. But I ken when there is a change in the air," she said decisively.

Lachlan quirked an eyebrow, wondering if perhaps those rumors about Mary MacManus being a kindly witch weren't based in truth. The rumors were mostly spread by village children who claimed to have seen her lugging a large cauldron out of the shed in her yard. One child insisted she saw Mary levitate over one of her chickens.

Witch or nae, she's a kind woman, and good to Rowan, he reminded himself, tipping his teacup back to catch every last sugary drop.

"So, Lachlan, Rowan tells me she saved yer life," Blair said, her voice loud enough to reach across the large table.

Lachlan and Mary both turned to look at Blair, who was staring at him with what looked like a challenge in her eyes.

'Tis a test, he realized instantly. *She wants to ken if I can admit to letting a lass fight for me life.*

"Aye, she did. She fought off six men and then tended to me wounds. She's a true marvel, me wife," Lachlan said, winking at Rowan, who immediately blushed at the praise.

Blair sat back, folding her arms, and dropping

her chin, a clear gesture of approbation. "Yer lucky to have her."

"Aye, and never a minute passes when I donnae think such," Lachlan said as he stood up.

"But I think 'tis time we go to the castle. We must talk to yer father," he said, holding a hand out to Rowan.

She took it, standing up and immediately coming to his side.

These actions alone, more than anything else that had happened between them this last week, revealed just how comfortable she had become in his presence.

She trusts me, and I will spend the rest of me life ensuring I end every day still worthy of that gift, he promised himself as he wrapped his fingers with hers, the warmth of her palm kissing the cool skin of his.

"Before ye go, I have something for ye," Mary MacManus said as she stood up, a subtle cracking emitting from her knees as she shuffled to one of the shelves at the far side of the cottage. The shelves were filled with glass jars containing what Lachlan could only assume were ingredients for her healing mixtures. Each glass jar was covered in a handwritten label, some of them so old the writing had nearly rubbed off.

He and Rowan watched as Mary reached up and selected a jar from the highest shelf and brought it back with her, handing it to Rowan.

"Ye healed that eye of his as good, or better than I would have done, but make sure ye use this every night on the broken rib. Active as ye are," Mary said, turning to Lachlan, "it will be harder for that area to heal, so this ought to keep ye from inflicting any more damage."

"How did ye—" Lachlan shook his head.

"A healer kens," Mary, Blair, and Rowan said in tandem, then the three burst into fresh peals of laughter.

"Thank ye, Mary. For yer kindness and the tea and cakes, which were the most delicious I have tasted. Though I would ask ye not to share that opinion with Cook..." Lachlan said, taking the jar from Mary's hands.

"Yes, thank ye, Mary," Rowan said, dropping Lachlan's hand to give the woman a hug.

Lachlan was struck by the familial way that Rowan acted with MacManuss, and he found himself glad to ken that in the absence of a mother, she had had Mary to guide her through life's more difficult moments.

"Donnae think that this ointment will cure ye of all yer ills right away. Ye need rest. More than ye think. A week away from the guard shifts ought to see ye right again," Mary lectured as she bustled them out of the door.

"Aye. I will do me best," Lachlan replied, knowing that while her advice was sound, there was little chance of him staying away from the guard for a week. It was in his bones to protect the castle and its people, and he would do so in whatever ways he could while his body healed.

"I shall meet ye here tomorrow, Blair," Rowan shouted over her shoulder.

Lachlan looked at her questioningly as they walked down the cottage's front path.

"We're going to pick the first bluebells to crush into powder. They're verra useful for wound healing," she said.

"Ye look happy, lass." Lachlan wrapped an arm around her and bringing her into his side.

"I am happy. I am home, with everyone I love nearby," she said, looking up at him. "It's all I've ever needed," she added, laying her head on his chest as they started up the small hill that led to the castle's side gate.

Lachlan closed his eyes and breathed in deeply, relishing the familiar air in his lungs, fresh with dewy grass and the clean tang of loch water.

"Are ye happy, Lachlan?" Rowan asked, bringing them to a stop at the top of the hill.

Lachlan looked down at his wife and grinned wide enough to look like a madman. "I have ye, lass. Ye are all I have ever wanted, and so yes, I am verra happy indeed."

EPILOGUE

Eighteen Months Later

"Two ankle sprains and a broken nose. What in God's name are ye teaching these lads, Lachlan? I swear they have nae sense in those brutish bodies," Rowan called as she stepped into the large stone house, setting her bag down on a table near the door and quickly divesting herself of her apron, cloak, and scarf.

The day had been blustery and cold, and her cheeks felt burned from the wind that had whipped at her from the moment she left the house at dawn to attend a birth and followed her all the way into the late afternoon when she had walked to the castle to tend to the newest round of guards.

When there was no answer to her outburst, she walked down the hall toward the kitchen, her favorite part of the house she and Lachlan now called home.

They had hired another of Ainslee's cousins, Violet, to make their meals, and the smell of Violet's signature lamb stew and fresh oat bread assaulted Rowan as she crossed the threshold into the large room.

Ainslee was seated at the table in the center of the room, one hand flipping through a book while the other rocked the cradle next to her back and forth.

"Where's Lachlan?" Rowan crossed the room to where her daughter was sleeping peacefully in the cradle.

"He's just returned from a ride with yer father. I expect he'll be down as soon as he changes out of his extremely muddy boots," Ainslee said, emphasizing the soiled state of her husband's footwear.

Rowan chuckled to herself. In many households, the staff was to be seen and not heard, but she enjoyed running her house as her mother and father had done, with maids and cooks and gardeners who felt like family. And, as in any family, there was a good amount of complaining to be done.

"If they're truly terrible, I'll make him clean them himself. He ought to use that polish Blair made for him anyway. She swears it repels dirt like nothing else," Rowan mused as she ran a finger ever so gently down her daughter's cheek.

Rinalda Stewart was, in Rowan's opinion, the prettiest bairn ever to be born in this part of Scotland. She had Lachlan's dark curls, Rowan's eyes, and, according to Rowan's father, the late Lady Campbell's lips, which could more often than not be found smiling even in her sleep.

Her entrance into Rowan and Lachlan's lives had been surprising but welcome. Rowan realized she was with child the night before they were due to make their way to Inverness, three months after their initial attempt at a honeymoon.

And when she realized that her nausea, headaches, and fatigue were the result not of the changing seasons or bad mutton but rather of the love she shared with her husband, she had immediately canceled their trip.

"I donnae wish to be on the road with ye, for we are about to embark on the life's greatest adventure, right here at Castle Morcoille," she had told Lachlan as she began unpacking their trunks.

Lachlan had been so elated at the news and

continued to be so in the ensuing months, growing as excited for their daughter as she was. He was the best father she could have hoped for their bairn, and she could not wait to tell him that now, she was with child again.

But in order to do so, she needed to see her husband, and so, reluctantly stepping away from her baby, she made her way up the stairs of their house.

It was a homely building less than a mile from the castle's eastern gate and had sat empty for the last ten years. Before, it was where Rowan's mother's family stayed when they visited, but three years after Lady Campbell died, so did her parents, and thus the house had stayed uninhabited ever since.

Her father had given her a selection of homes from which to choose, but as soon as she stepped foot in Heather House, as it was called, she had been hit with a certainty that this was where she and Lachlan would raise their family. Living in a space her connected even tangentially to her mother helped Rowan feel a tie to the woman she knew so little about, and the house was just private enough to allow her and Lachlan to feel they were living their lives, not as the daughter and son-in-law of the laird, but as two villagers trying to fashion a humble life for themselves.

They were treated as such, with neighbors stopping in to see Rinalda, share honey, or ask Lachlan's help with animal skinning. Though they often ventured to the castle for meals and functions, Rowan enjoyed the separation between her life and that of the castle. It allowed her the space to be herself, to live her life with Lachlan exactly as they wished it.

As Rowan reached the last stair, she looked out the window directly across from her, which offered a beautiful view of the forest, where she, Lachlan, and now Rinalda spent so much time. Time spent gathering herbs and flowers with Blair now also included Rinalda, wrapped tightly against Rowan's chest. As she picked and pruned, Rowan told her daughter the names—Latin and English—of the greenery that filled her basket.

Rinalda wasn't speaking yet, but her mumbles had begun to take on a distinctly botanical sound, as though her mouth was struggling to form the words she heard Blair and Rowan so often mutter.

Rowan and Lachlan hunted together whenever they could, and last Christmas, he had gifted her with her very own archery target, set back in a secluded area of the woods where each morning she went to practice.

"Rowan? Is that ye I hear?" Lachlan's voice called from their bedroom.

Rowan turned a corner and walked into the room they shared to find her husband with one boot off and the other very much still stuck on and covered in muck and leaves. She laughed at the sight of her strong man struggling with something so silly as a boot and bent down before him, shooing away his hand.

With one swift tug, she removed the shoe and set it by her side, careful not to place it on the rug where it could stain.

"Och, thank ye, lass. Ye've nae idea how I've tarried with that. I've been stuck quite literally in those boots since sunup," he said, glaring at the shoes as he offered her his hand and pulled her into his lap.

"But no matter," he said, turning back to her. "How is me wife today? I heard ye shouting downstairs, but not well enough to ken what ye were saying."

"I was scolding ye for yer guards' injuries—three in one day. What in God's name are ye putting them through in training?" she asked with a laugh.

"They're young and donnae yet ken their own limits. And I plan to make this new set of guards the strongest yet. I will nae have any more attacks on me watch."

It was said in jest, of course. Castle Morcoille and its inhabitants had experienced nary a nuisance since Andrew MacDonald's attack on Rowan and Lachlan more than a year ago. Rowan's father had sent the MacDonalds a letter that, while not entirely threatening, had stated if they did not begin to earn their money the honest way, he would pull his support from their mills, their only means of support.

Since then, the MacDonalds had stayed in their corner of Scotland and, according to Rowan's father, had not one but four thriving mills and twenty acres of oats that were producing enough to keep not only the laird and his son fed but their tenants as well. Andrew was still unwed, but he had not tried to steal another lass from her husband in order to augment his coffers. Rumor had it that he ran the mill much of the time and had become a rather adept local baker known for his sour oatcakes, best enjoyed with bramble jam.

He had sent Castle Morcoille's cook the recipe as a form of apology for trying to work his charm on one of her kitchen maids, but Cook had burned it almost immediately.

"My oatcakes are from a recipe perfected over three generations. I'm nae switching to a new formula just because some arrogant fool says so," Cook had thundered.

"Be easy with the lads," Rowan said now of the young guards. "I cannae spend me entire time healing them. I have much else to tend to. In fact, just today, I found something that will occupy much of me time over the next few months," she said, unable to keep the excitement from her voice.

Lachlan noticed it instantly, sitting up straighter and looking at her with anticipation as he said, "And what might that be?"

Rowan took his hand and placed it on her still-flat belly. "Another one of your bairns. Due in a few months, I believe, and with any luck, a boy."

Lachlan jumped to his feet and hugged Rowan tightly, though his grip was far less so around her belly, already caring for the tiny seed inside her.

He whooped with joy as he walked out of the room and down the stairs in his bare feet, his laughter so loud that soon, it was joined by the sound of Rinalda's screeching, awakened from her peaceful slumber.

"Ye've woken the wee bairn," Rowan scolded him, though, in truth, she did not mind. Her daughter would have to get used to the noise, for the house had ten rooms if she did not count hers, Lachlan's, and the maids' rooms, and she planned to fill each one with a child.

"I cannae be silent, Rowan. Already each day ye make me the happiest of men, but today, I think ye have outdone yerself," he said, setting her down at the bottom of the stairs and bringing his hands to her cheeks.

His eyes bore through hers, a stare that a year ago would have sent her running, but now, brought warmth to her body and joy to her heart.

"I love ye, Lachlan Stewart, and I am verra glad that ye are me husband," she whispered, placing her hands atop his.

"And I ye, Rowan Campbell. I'll be forever grateful ye chose me," he told her.

A HIGHLANDER'S CAPTIVE

Book One of the Highland Temptations Series!

Captivity was only the beginning...

Rufus MacIntosh wants his family's birthright back. He's fought wars and his own personal demons. Time to claim what is his family's. More specifically, his brother's. And so, bringing friends and allies, he takes back what is his family's. The lands are theirs again. Except now, Rufus discovers his brother has abandoned the birthright, the land, all of this. He's headed to new lands and new worlds.

Rufus should be relieved, he's no longer responsible for any of it. He can walk away from their ancestral lands. He's not sure if he wants to.

Davina MacFarland never claimed she was an angel. She certainly isn't a common thief, even though she's related to one, now that her brother took Rufus McIntosh's lands. She shouldn't have been involved. She really shouldn't. But now there's been a scuffle and she's the captive of that damned Rufus MacIntosh. But she can hold her own. Or can she?

CHAPTER 1

For hundreds of years, much longer than the man in the red and green tartan had been alive, the MacIntosh Clan made their home along the banks of Moray Firth. Men had been born, lived, and died there. They'd wed their women, sired their bairns, fought and laughed and even wept when the occasion called for it.

When it was time to war, the men went without questioning the reason for it, and were brave and true to their clan and its chiefs. They fought large and small wars, wars against the crown and wars against opposing clans. No one could state with complete certainty when and where the ancient feud with the Cameron Clan had begun, truth be told, but that had been put to rest after more than three hundred years. Hundreds of years in which men had fought and died for the glory of their clan, all because their ancestors had done the same.

The man in the red and green tartan sat astride a chestnut gelding outside the tavern in Perth. A tavern which he knew held the men he was looking for. He hadn't seen them since they'd parted ways after the disaster that was Culloden and had leapt at the chance to join up with them again when his friend William Blackheath had suggested them for this mission.

Good men, fearsome warriors. But then so many had been fearsome, had they not? Perhaps it was merely luck or fate which had spared him, and these men recommended by William when others were long since dead and gone.

Not a part of his life he enjoyed looking back on. No man wanted to be on the losing side of a war. But the war was over—at least, the war between the Jacobites and the loyalists.

His war had begun more recently, while he fought on the side of Bonnie Prince Charlie. When in the course of a single night, his family's fortune had turned upside-down, and with no way to protect those he loved—and that which his family had devoted centuries—to without being branded a deserter.

Men had deserted, those who'd concluded that there would be no winning. They had not been treated well.

The row of horses and carts tied in front of the tavern in the center of Perth would have been enough to tell him how crowded it was inside without the sounds of so many male voices raised in what could only be a fight. He heaved a put-upon sigh before striding through the door.

He immediately stepped aside as a man with a bloodied nose soared past, out into a puddle of sludge which Rufus MacIntosh had been fortunate enough to avoid. He cringed when gray water splashed out in all directions.

Not much had changed since his last visit.

"Come on, then!" a booming voice cried.

Rufus looked across the large, packed room in time to see his cousin Drew waving the next chal-lenger his way. One of his eyes had already swollen shut and his lower lip dripped blood onto his chin. The knuckles of his raised fist were bruised and stained with yet more blood—though Rufus suspected it was not his own.

He jerked his chin upward, tossing back his head

and the sweat-soaked dark hair hanging over his forehead. He'd fought more than his share already that day, it seemed.

A man built roughly like a tree stood before Drew, his kin cheering him on from behind. Tall enough that he'd likely needed to duck when entering the tavern, and as wide as two men standing shoulder-to-shoulder, his bald head nearly touched the lanterns hanging from the ceiling. Drew was only half the man's size and had likely drunk his weight in ale, yet he did not back down. It wasn't in his nature.

In fact, he urged the much larger opponent to come at him. "I haven't all day, man!" he jeered, waving the giant on again.

The giant charged, roaring as he did, and a cheer went up over the swaying, laughing, wagering men standing in a ring around them.

The giant threw his arms out to the sides, intending to grab Drew up in a bear hug, but the smaller, quicker man ducked him. He then leaped straight up, throwing an arm around the giant's thick neck and landing a series of sharp, stinging jabs to the side of his opponent's head.

The giant threw himself back against the wall in hopes of crushing Drew, drawing an outraged scream from old Brodric. "Och, dinna break my walls! I'll take the mortar outta yer bones!"

Drew held on, which was not a surprise to Rufus. His cousin had been a scrapper from birth, moments from death when he slid from his mother's womb and into the world. As legend had it, Isla MacIntosh had reached for the slick babe between her legs, held her bairn upside down by his ankles and tapped his back until a hunk of mucus had flown out, and he'd taken his first breath before squalling his lungs out.

He'd been fighting ever since.

Drew locked his arms around that thick neck, squeezing until the giant's face turned red—then, a shade of violet. He dropped to his knees, beating at the arms cutting off his air, but Rufus knew what the giant didn't.

He'd been at the receiving end of his cousin's ministrations enough times to know there was no making Drew quit. Not until he was good and satisfied.

When the man's eyes slid shut, and he fell forward like a tree falling before the ax, a mighty cheer went up over those in the tavern who'd wagered on Drew MacIntosh's unflagging determination. Only a fool would wager against him.

"That's enough, that's enough!" Brodric shouted. "Ye have made enough of a wreck of the place for one day, Drew, and ye know it."

Drew stumbled to his feet, a smile stretching from ear to ear. "Ye know I'll give ye some of my winnings, man. Quit making such a fuss. Ye remind me of my mam."

"Your mam woulda been smart to knock yer head against a wall twice a day to force some sense into ye." Brodric handed Drew a mug nearly over-flowing with ale.

"She did. How do ye think I am the way I am?" Drew drank deeply, emptying the mug before drag-ging the back of his arm across his mouth.

Rufus clapped his cousin's shoulder. "I should have known I'd find ye breaking the place up when I arrived."

"Och, what took ye so long, then?" Drew asked, looking him up and down. "I thought ye forgot where to find this run-down pit."

"A run-down pit ye all but live in," Brodric grum-bled. "Tis good enough for ye nearly every day of the week."

"Aye, and the thirsty men who hang about the place to watch me make a fool of myself work up a terrible thirst, do they not?" Drew slammed the mug into Brodric's waiting hand and turned his full attention to Rufus. "So. Are ye ready to be on about your business, then?"

"Aye. Have ye gathered the men William recommended for the job?"

William Blackheath, commander of the guard of a great Highland laird, was unable to shirk his duties in order to assist his friend, even when the stakes were so high, but he had suggested men he was certain would provide Rufus the skill and strength he would need on his side.

"Aye. Ye just watched one of them fight." Drew jerked his head toward the man still coming to his senses, fighting his way to his feet after regaining consciousness. The giant.

"Him?" Rufus gaped. "Ye canna mean it."

"Aye."

"The one ye just put to sleep? That's your idea of fighting?"

"Listen to me, lad. Men tend to look at the likes of Clyde McMannis and run the other way rather than come to blows. We'd have that in our favor. And not every man is as fearsome a fighter as myself, ye ken. Not every man would find it as easy to take the beast down."

"Och, of course." Rufus rolled his eyes at his

cousin's boasting. "That's all very well and good, but who else have ye?"

"Aside from Clyde, there's Tyrone Robertson and Alec Abernathy. Ye know them to be fine fighters."

"Aye," Rufus nodded in appreciation. "Tyrone came between me and one of Cumberland's men back at Inverness. I'd be food for the worms at this very moment if it were not for him."

"And he'll likely never allow ye to forget it," Drew grinned.

"I intend to make certain ye all have what you're owed when this is over, and my family's land has been restored," he vowed. "Ye know Kenneth is a fair man, and he'll be even more indebted to all of ye than myself once he's where he belongs."

Kenneth MacIntosh, oldest son of Elliot MacIntosh, was by rights the man entitled to the land his father and the seven men preceding him had worked and lived and died on. Their bones rested in that very earth, bones buried centuries earlier. Yet, Kenneth been driven away while his younger brother, the only other living son, had been fighting an ill-fated war.

Drew's face hardened from its usual lighthearted expression into one of deadly seriousness. "Ye know this means more to me than a sporran full of jingling coin," he muttered. "This is my family's honor at stake as much as it is yours. We'll see that bastard MacFarland hung up by his heels and flayed alive for what he did."

Someone called for Drew then, and he patted Rufus's arm before leaving him alone. Though one could never truly be alone when in a crowded tavern, jostled about, ears ringing.

Yet he might as well have been standing in the center of a deserted glen for all they meant to him just then. His thoughts were far away, years in the past. He'd been in Glenfinnan when word had arrived of the horrors his family had endured, and not a day had passed in the year since then, that Rufus had not sworn vengeance on the man who'd destroyed everything he'd left behind.

If there was one thing Ian MacFarland had done right, it was performing his evil deeds while Rufus was away and could not bear witness.

"So, you've taken it into yer head to kill Ian MacFarland, then?" Brodric asked with a knowing jerk of his chin.

"Aye. I have that," Rufus confirmed for all who would hear. Best for the man to know it, if any of them took it into their heads to spread the word. He wanted Ian to know. Wanted him to look over his shoulder whenever he so much as stepped away to make water in private. "I'll kill him if it comes to it, though what I want is my land. My family's land. My brother's birthright. He might not be able to fight for it himself, but then, he's not a fighting man such as I."

"He took a terrible blow at MacFarland's hand that day, from what I heard," Brodric mused. "He might have gone the way of—"

"Aye," Rufus acknowledged before the man could continue. He was a full-grown man who'd seen hundreds die, perhaps thousands, yet there were things he couldn't stand to hear. Such as the tale of his parents' murder.

"Aye, and what else, then?" The old man fixed him with a shrewd eye. There was no lying to him, no telling half-truths. He'd seen more than enough in his many years riding through the Highlands to know the truth of a man's heart.

Rufus gave a half-shrug. One that meant nothing, and gave nothing away.

"Would that I were a younger man," Brodric lamented as he poured a flagon of ale. "I would ride at your side straight into hell if it meant avenging Elliot MacIntosh. A finer man never lived, and that's a fact."

"Aye, that it is," Rufus agreed.

"And your mother, rest her sainted soul. The loveliest thing I ever set eyes on when she was a girl. Most women dinna look as pleasing as the years pass, ye ken, but she was one of the exceptions. Bonnier with each passing day, and woe to the man who believed her nothing but a lovely face, for she could wield a sword, and later a pistol, as well as nearly any man."

"That, she could," Rufus chuckled, his mood turning at the memory. Would that she'd wielded a weapon against Ian MacFarland and knocked his worthless, murdering, thieving head from his shoulders before he'd brought an end to her.

Rufus could not even visit the place where his parents' bodies were laid to rest. There was no setting foot on the land without possibly losing that foot.

That wouldn't keep him away forever.

Yes, Ian MacFarland would be wise to look over his shoulder wherever he went. He could not keep Rufus from exacting the revenge his family so richly deserved, revenge he'd dreamed of every time his eyes closed.

CHAPTER 2

It should not have come as such a surprise that Clyde's horse was so very large.

"The thing's a monster." Tyrone scratched his head, making his red hair stand up on end before he pulled a blue tam over it, covering him to the ears. "I didna know they made horses so… massive."

"He needs a larger horse than most, I suppose," Rufus shrugged. "I'd expect to find this beast pulling a cart."

"Or a house," Tyrone posed. "He could likely pull a house."

"Likely. Do ye know him? Clyde?"

Tyrone shook his head. "Drew said he does not talk much. He doesn't need to, I would imagine. He lets his size speak for him."

This was hardly a problem in Rufus's eyes, as he had never cared for people whose tongues were hung in the middle and swung freely all day. They would ride together for at least a fortnight, perhaps longer, if MacFarland and his kin managed to avoid capture.

The thought of listening to nonstop talking made his skin crawl.

"We need to move," he reminded Drew, who stepped out of the tavern with bags loaded over both arms.

"Do ye fancy the notion of riding out with no food, lad? Or drink?" Drew chuckled as he hung the bags from the saddle of his gelding, whose hooves pawed impatiently at the ground.

"Dinna pretend it's the food ye care about," Rufus smirked. "And it isn't as if we canna hunt."

"Perhaps ye can," Drew shrugged, swinging his compact body up onto the gelding's back. "Ye know I was never much with a bow. And this is only a day's worth, perhaps two. I didna see reason for us to start with nothing. A few extra minutes will not make a bit of difference."

Rufus bit back a sharp reply. Perhaps it meant nothing to his cousin, but he had all but counted the minutes since he'd received word of his parents' death and his brother's removal from his rightful place. Every minute more was like an eternity.

What must it look like to Drew, and especially to the others? They were not of his blood, they had no reason outside of the gold which Rufus had promised in return for their services to endanger their lives. And their lives would indeed be in danger if Ian MacFarland had a chance to make it so.

The pitiful excuse for a man would murder a pair of old people in their very home. He was capable of any sort of devilry.

Yet none of them seemed concerned in the least about the possible danger. In fact, they welcomed it.

"Come on, then." Alec's obsidian eyes sparkled with excitement. "I'm longing to sink my dirk into the flesh of a murderous bastard or two."

"Aye," Tyrone agreed as he hauled his considerably powerful body onto the back of an equally powerful horse. Nothing compared to Clyde's draft horse, but still impressive.

His eyes widened when he took note of the tartan half-hidden beneath Rufus's cloak, wrapped across his chest and torso and tucked into his kilt. The dim lighting inside the tavern accounted for his not having noticed earlier. Now, in full daylight, the sun nearly overhead, it was plain to see. "Ye believe it's wise to wear that?" he murmured.

Rufus looked down at the colorful sash. His family's tartan, green on a field of red. "Aye. I do. Let any man challenge my right to do so."

"Ye know it's against the law now. Unless a man's a member of the army."

"I know it." Rufus met his gaze with an equally steady eye. "And as I said, let any man challenge me."

"I merely wished to be certain," Tyrone shrugged. "Ye know such matters have never mattered much to me."

Rufus looked around at the other men. "If any of ye have a concern over my wearing the MacIntosh tartan, speak now. I would not wish to put any of ye in danger against your wishes."

Drew snorted, bringing his gelding about. "Come on, then. I thought ye were in a rush to get moving."

"I'm selling my sword in your service," Alec reminded him. "Do ye think it matters to me what ye wear?"

Clyde spoke not a word. He merely grunted, nodded, and took the reins in hand.

"All right, then." They started off northwest, where

Brodric reported that the MacFarlands would ride after returning to their ancestral land to gather supplies. They'd ridden straight back to Moray Firth, back to the home in which Rufus had spent his earliest days.

It would be where the MacFarlands spent their last.

IT WAS NEAR DARK, only the faintest beams of struggling sunlight sliding through overhanging birch branches, when Rufus spotted something in the woods to his right.

He'd been riding at the front of the group for half the day by that point, clutching his cloak closed against the chill which grew more pronounced the lower the sun sank. It would be a damp, cool night, with a fire necessary to keep the men warm while they slept.

He was considering this while Alec and Tyrone compared tales of the various lasses they'd bedded between battles and was just about to bring up the fact that they'd need to make camp before long when another, different noise caught his attention.

His head snapped around in that direction in

time to catch sight of a moving lump against a gnarled old trunk.

Rufus brought the horse to a halt and held up a hand to stop the others, his gaze trained on the spot where he'd observed the movement.

"Ye saw something?" Drew murmured when he reached his side.

A slight nod of his head before dismounting, eyes still directed to the place where someone or something watched them. One hand on the hilt of his claymore, he took a few steps in the direction of the moving mass, nothing about it giving him the impression of it being human.

Until it coughed.

"Who are ye?" Rufus leveled his steel at the hunched figure while he was still several steps away. "Speak. Tell me who ye are and what ye happen to be doing here."

The figure moved. "That's two questions. Which of the two would ye prefer I answer first?"

The voice was not that of a man.

"Who is it?" Alec shouted behind him.

"I canna say as yet," Rufus called back.

"I can say." The figure shifted again, the hood of the brown cloak sliding down to reveal a mass of loose-hanging auburn curls just visible in the dim light. "Though I won't, because it happens to be no business of yours."

A woman. She would not be alone. Rufus looked around, sword still at the ready—the lass could easily conceal a weapon beneath that cloak of hers, and it would hardly be the first time a group of cutthroats used a woman as a lure to attract foolish men.

The woods appeared empty and sounded that way, too, but it meant nothing for a group of skilled thieves or murderers to remain silent and still.

"Who are ye with?" he demanded, still speaking to the back of her head.

"Myself. No one else." She turned, glaring at him with what looked like two blazing coals set in a face devoid of color. "And I'll thank ye to get that sword out of my face. Do I look like I'm in any position to attack ye? Or are ye just that afraid of a woman, on her own and injured, in the middle of the woods with no horse or food or anything to sustain her that ye feel the need to threaten her? Is that it?"

He stared in frank, open-mouthed surprise. Yes, she appeared to be weak, in spite of the fire in her voice. Hungry—those blazing eyes of hers were sunk deep into her face, ringed in what looked like bruises but was likely the result of starvation.

It mattered little. Not at all, in fact. What mattered was keeping his men safe. Not to mention himself.

"I'll lower the sword when I'm certain ye have no weapons, lass, and not a minute sooner. Can ye walk?"

"What is it to ye?" she challenged. "Unless ye intend to help me, I have little cause to work my way to my feet and prove myself to ye."

"For one who looks as though she is in need of help, ye have a wicked tongue. If I were to offer ye assistance, ye would need to get up. I don't much fancy the notion of crouching alongside ye."

Two bright red spots of color flamed on her cheeks. "It's just as well, as I don't recall asking for assistance."

"Ye obviously prefer to starve, then," he sneered, growing more confident by the moment that the woman was indeed on her own and indeed no sort of threat to him. This hardly meant that he would fall before her and offer her his protection—especially when she had such a nasty manner.

"Perhaps I do, if my other choice is to spend so much as a minute with the likes of ye," she snarled in return, going so far as to bare her teeth.

"Enjoy starvation, then." He backed away rather

than turning his back on her, still wary of what she might be concealing. She scoffed, seeming to curl in on herself, tucked inside the cradle of gnarled roots.

Alec still waited for him. "Who is it?"

"A beast from hell, if ye want the truth of it," Rufus growled. "A woman."

Wide eyes beneath the brim of his tam. "A woman? Alone?"

"She appeared to be. Also appeared to be injured. Would not rise from her position and wouldn't accept assistance when I offered."

"Ye offered? Truly?" Alec fixed him with a gaze that could only be described as skeptical. "From where I stood and what I overheard, ye hardly sounded helpful. Ye sounded threatening."

"Was I supposed to carry her to safety?" Rufus scoffed as he sheathed his sword. "That's not going to happen, my friend."

Alec looked over his shoulder, a frown creasing his forehead. "I dinna much like the thought of leaving an unarmed woman to the mercy of whatever comes along. I know ye dinna, either. Tis going to be a cold night, and that's a fact. I don't much like the thought of my conscience plaguing me."

"Nay, but there's nothing to be done for her if she's too daft to get up and come along."

A rustling noise caused him to spin in place, and his surprise at finding himself face-to-face with the thin, pale, fierce woman with eyes the color of steel that somehow burned into him, saw through him, and did not like what they found. "I can stand. Here I am."

Yet she leaned against the nearest tree, and her left leg was slightly bent to allow her foot to hover over the ground. The soft leather boot she wore on her right foot was not present on her left.

"What happened to ye?" Alec asked, nudging his way past Rufus that he might have a better view.

"Fell from the saddle," she grunted. "Something spooked the mare. She threw me."

"She ran, then?"

"Aye." In that single word was a world of disappointment, frustration, exhaustion.

"And ye were alone out here?" Rufus asked.

She shifted her weight somewhat, that she was standing upright—if still only on one foot. "What is it to ye whether or not I was alone? Why must ye keep asking? I'm alone now. That's what matters, is it not?"

He opened his mouth, ready to challenge her, but Alec spoke first. "It's right ye are, lass. Dinna worry. I suppose ye have not been able to tend to your injury, then."

She softened, shaking her head with a resigned sigh. "I dinna think it's broken, as I can move my toes, but it swelled so, I had to remove my boot, and there's no chance of getting it back on."

Alec glanced at Rufus. The two of them held an entire silent conversation over the course of a few moments.

Rufus sighed his frustration, then looked about in all directions. "I suppose this is as good a place as any to make camp for the night, though I would prefer we work our way further from the road."

"I'll tell the others," Alec announced, leaving Rufus with the woman.

Exactly where he didn't wish to be.

I hope you enjoyed this Aileen Adams work!

For more Aileen Adams works, click here!

Sign up for the newsletter to be notified of new releases.

Click on link for
Newsletter
or put this in your browser window:
mailerlite.com/webforms/landing/o3j5x0

www.ingramcontent.com/pod-product-compliance
Lightning Source LLC
Chambersburg PA
CBHW020328160726
47992CB00004B/1741

* 9 7 9 8 4 6 1 6 8 2 5 5 2 *